T0095143

THE MYSTERY OF THE WOODEN CRATE

The Steve Mitchell Adventure Series
Volume 2

RICK OATES

Order this book online at www.trafford.com
or email orders@trafford.com

Most Trafford titles are also available at major online book retailers.

Author Credits: Edited by Dawni Arias and Amanda Cantrell

Printed in the United States of America.

ISBN: 978-1-4269-5962-2 (sc)
ISBN: 978-1-4269-5963-9 (hc)
ISBN: 978-1-4269-5964-6 (e)

Library of Congress Control Number: 2011903075

Trafford rev. 03/11/2011

www.trafford.com

North America & international
toll-free: 1 888 232 4444 (USA & Canada)
phone: 250 383 6864 • fax: 812 355 4082

Disclaimer

This is a work of fiction. Any similarity to persons living or dead, locations, actions, or other world activities, past or present, is merely coincidental.

This book is dedicated to my ultimate hero in life…my Dad. The one who taught me the Biblical precepts of working hard, dreaming big, diligent prayer and to expect results.

Thanks Dad…I love you.

CHAPTER 1

St Paul, Minnesota
Present Day – 9:00 a.m.

Steve slowly opened the door to his office with his coffee cup in hand. He peered into the room he had not seen for quite awhile. He had spent his time recuperating from the injuries he received from the crash of his Cessna 310 aircraft weeks earlier.

On the corner of his desk sat a stack of unopened mail. He thought about the last time he was in his office and how simple his life was back then. Due to the recent turn of events, he now faced a multitude of questions. Questions he could not easily answer.

He moved to the bookshelf in the corner that housed various medals and commendations he received while in the service. He cleared a shelf in the middle of the display. Steve set his briefcase on the corner of the shelf and opened it.

Carefully, from the briefcase he pulled a wooden carving of a Cessna 310 aircraft with the identification numbers *1144Q* carved on the fuselage. The wood the sculpture was carved from testified of its approximate 140 year-old age. He placed the fragile wooden sculpture on the shelf he had just cleared. Behind the carving he placed a picture frame that contained a drawing of an airplane and its inscription, *To Tommy, Steve Mitchell 1863*. It was his only connection to a remarkable experience. Although it was a long time ago, it still seemed like it was yesterday.

Steve's story was amazing. It was an experience that was hard to understand but somehow it happened. In a strange warp of the unexplained, he had miraculously gone back in time, fell in love with a schoolteacher in the 1860's, and at the same time influenced his great grandfather as a little boy. Then just as mysteriously as the time travel had happened, he suddenly returned to the present.

He originally thought it was a dream until he pulled that piece of paper from the miniature carving of a Cessna 310 aircraft found in his great-grandfather's treasure chest. It testified to Steve's influence in his great grandfather's life to place hope in the future. It was at that moment Steve realized the experience was real but he still could not explain how it happened.

He had a hard time accepting the fact that he actually influenced his family into the aircraft industry. It was almost too much to comprehend; that he met his great-grandfather Tommy back in 1863, when his great-grandfather was just a boy.

Nevertheless, it happened. He had to move on with his life. He could not think about Tommy, Jean, or the rest of the people in the life he built back in the 1860's. He had to accept it as something in life that cannot be explained.

After opening his great-grandfather's treasure chest and finding a number of fortunes, it was decided by the family to keep just a few heirlooms and sell off the stocks and bonds also found. They were worth a fortune.

The family would never discuss the actual amount but it was evident no one was hurting financially. Steve had the funds to do anything he wanted. However, he was determined not to let his newfound fortune go to his head. Instead, he would use it to better his already thriving charter business.

He sat at his desk and placed his hands on the desktop. He eerily stared at the notes lying there that he had scratched weeks earlier from a phone call he had received.

He saw the names of *George McClure* and *Rich Versetti* scribbled on his desk pad. The names loomed large in his mind. They were a mystery now. Who were they and why was Steve hired to ferry that wooden crate to California?

The crate was found in the wreckage of Steve's plane but it was empty. The contents of the crate were still a mystery. He only knew what he was told. The wooden crate was to have contained a rare African artifact but Steve could not confirm that. The crate was heavily banded and locked when it was delivered to him at his office.

Steve slid open the middle desk drawer. On top of the various collection of paperclips, pens, and rubber bands lay a piece of scratch paper Steve had scribbled on the last time he was at his desk. It read – *George McClure (916)555-4638*. He picked up the note and slowly closed the drawer while staring at the piece of paper. Steve wondered who he was and if he knew anything about the mysterious crate.

Steve decided he was going to have to start piecing this whole ordeal together. After all, he had the $75,000 he was paid to deliver the crate to California but it never even made it out of the state of Minnesota. Furthermore, the contents of the crate turned up missing in the wreckage of his Cessna 310 aircraft.

Steve picked up the phone and listened for a dial tone. He dialed the number written on the scratch paper for George McClure and waited for whomever to pick up the receiver on the other end. There was no answer. Instead, the phone was answered with a recording.

"We're sorry but you have reached a number that has been disconnected. No further information is available for 9-1-6-5-5-5-4-6-3-8."

Bewildered, Steve hung up the phone. The number was his only connection to George McClure who hired him to take that crate to California. He picked up the phone again and called information.

"AT&T, may I help you?" The telephone operator asked.

"Yes, the number for R&D Productions in San Francisco, California please," Steve responded.

"One moment please…still checking."

After a short pause, the operator told Steve there was no listing for R&D Productions in or around the San Francisco area.

Again, Steve placed the phone receiver back into its cradle. He pondered what to do next. He opened his laptop computer and did an internet search for R & D Productions. He found a few listings for companies that began with R & D but none of them had anything to do with productions. Searching the name of George McClure yielded too many results. Without a city and state, he could not pinpoint a specific region to search.

The insurance company would not cover any part of the crate because Steve could not furnish documentation of what it contained. He finally decided that he would just have to wait for Mr. McClure to contact him, whoever he was and wherever he was from.

Steve stuck the note back into his drawer as the phone rang. Steve quickly reached for it. He was anticipating a phone call hoping to solve the mystery of that crate.

"Mitchell's Executive Thrill Charter, may I help you?"

After a long absence, Steve felt good about answering the phone again. He had returned to work, ready to do business once more. He was ready to get back in the groove of running his business.

"Hey Steve, glad to have you back in the saddle. This is Frank from the control tower. So, how ya doing?"

"Hi Frank. It's great to hear your voice. I'm still a little sore but it's getting better. Thanks for asking."

"Great to hear things are...*looking up*."

Both men chuckled sheepishly with Frank's attempt at humor. Frank never was much of an outgoing person. Rather, he was kind of a nerdy fellow.

"Say Steve, as you know, I was working the tower the day you crashed and I just thought of something. When it happened, I didn't think it to be strange but now I wonder. Shortly after you took off, a Jet Ranger helicopter followed you out of our airspace. Right after your crash, it dropped off our radar then reappeared about ten minutes later. I didn't think anything of it at the time. After all, it's a helicopter."

"Do you remember the *N* number?" Steve asked.

"All I can remember was *N24* something or other. The only reason it sticks in my mind is that it was registered in California. At that time I thought to myself, *that chopper sure was a long way from home*."

Steve's interest was kindled because he was flying the crate to California. He wondered if there was a connection between the two.

Steve asked Frank, "Do you think you can look at your records and get me the full *N* number and the registered owner?"

"No can do buddy. The NTSB confiscated our records for their investigation. If I get them back soon, I'll call and let you know."

"Thanks Frank. Hey listen, I gotta run. Thanks again for the info."

"No problem Steve. Let's get together for lunch soon. Martha at the North Pole Café has sure missed your smiling face dropping in for morning coffee."

"Sounds good Frank…soon, okay, later."

"Nice talking with ya Steve."

Steve slowly hung up the phone. His mind was deep in thought. He wondered what kind of connection, if any, that helicopter had with the disappearance of the crates contents.

Surely someone was going to start questioning what happened. He was paid $75,000 to transfer supposed African artifacts to California but they never made it. People do not take kindly to not delivering, especially when they pay you in cash.

Steve sipped a drink of his now cold coffee. He picked up the phone and dialed the number for Julie. She was the nurse that was at his bedside during his comatose stay at the hospital. Throughout the ordeal, both had become good friends. From the first day he heard her speak, he had a feeling they had met before but he just could not place the connection.

"Hello," Julie answered.

"Well, if it isn't little Miss Nurse Julie. I thought I was dialing the dry cleaners," Steve jokingly said.

Julie giggled as she returned the sarcasm.

"Why it is the cleaners Mr. Steve, and I'm sorry to inform you but you had better bring a lot of money for dinner tonight. The reason being...I'm hungry, and ready to clean up on your wallet."

Steve laughingly answered, "Oh I'm sorry, I must have dialed the wrong number."

"Oh, I got your number Mr. Mitchell," Julie replied.

Both chuckled again. The bond of friendship that was formed between the two started long before Steve even knew her name. Julie had such compassion when he was lying in a vegetative state at the hospital. She was constantly at his side attending to him.

After a few minutes of small talk he told her he would pick her up at 7:00 p.m. They would have dinner at Steve's favorite restaurant, The Tin-Shawn-Day. It was located in Newport, MN and not far from the North Pole Café. The older establishment had made a name for themselves with their specialty; deep-fried Atlantic cod. Steve would visit as often as his schedule allowed.

Newport, Minnesota
That Night - 6:58 p.m.

Shortly before 7:00 p.m. that evening Steve arrived at Julie's house. He sat in his car momentarily thinking of her. She came into his life in such a strange way, a difficult manner nonetheless, but still compassionately. Her caring nature caused Steve to grow fond of her in a loving way.

He opened his car door and headed for her front steps with a spring in his walk. Julie peered out the living room window and saw him approaching her door.

She thought how handsome he was. He walked with a rugged yet adorable swagger. He looked so different from when she first met him. She knew he was different the first day he was rolled into the emergency room, battered and beaten from the crash. She had a heartfelt connection that she just could not place.

Steve met Julie already bounding down the steps. He turned and put his arm out so she could interlock hers with his. They strolled down the sidewalk, arm in arm, while bantering back and forth in a playful way.

Before opening the passenger door for her, he turned her inward and kissed her lips while placing his hands gently on her cheeks. It was that kiss where she first felt the bond of friendship growing into something much deeper. Her heart toiled wondering where she could place the feelings she experienced with such a delicate kiss.

At dinner they discussed Steve's phone call from Frank in the tower. Both were equally intrigued as to whether the information from the phone call had any significance in solving the mystery of the empty crate.

As the evening progressed, Julie questioned Steve how his search was going in finding the warplane he wanted to purchase for his aircraft fleet. He told her he had a couple of ads he was looking at and would probably check out one or two in the next couple of days. He said the first one he wanted to see was a *Curtiss Helldiver* bomber advertised in the Lake Tahoe, CA area. He never came out and invited her and she joked with him about it. Julie adored the Tahoe area.

They finished their dinner and walked out to the restaurant patio to enjoy the night air. They stood with arms interlocked while gazing at the nighttime sky.

"Steve?" Julie asked.

"With what you have gone through, with the crash and the back in time thing…has it changed, I mean, really changed the person you are?"

Before answering Steve paused to gather his thoughts. He spoke softly.

"Yes, it has changed me. It has brought the meaning of life so much closer. Today we have phones, internet, instant messaging, you name it…we have it. I mean we are so connected to the world and people's views that it's downright scary. We have the entire world readily available at our fingertips.

"Nevertheless, you know what? No matter what the world can produce that rushes information at us, there is not a product out there that can rush love. Love takes place in the heart. Two people must connect by their hearts to love. It does not need gadgets and information. It just needs two hearts. It's been the same throughout the ages. It does not matter what year it is, who it is, or nationality they are…it is the same.

"That's what's changed about me. Yeah, I still use this world's gadgets to get through life. But when it comes to loving others, the only instrument I have is my heart."

Julie just smiled at him. Her feelings were warmed. She snuggled up to his side and let his words linger in her heart. She felt comforted just being with Steve.

They finished the night the way it began. A warm, sweet, simple kiss that was as gentle as the evening breeze.

CHAPTER 2

Lake Tahoe Airport, California
One Week Later - Thursday 2:00 p.m. (PST)

Steve arrived at the Lake Tahoe Airport in response to an aircraft ad in the area. He had searched the internet for quite some time from his St. Paul, MN charter service office for just the right plane. He was determined to purchase another aircraft before the end of the year for tax purposes. The Lake Tahoe ad was the first he decided to pursue.

The *Curtiss SB2C Helldiver* aircraft captured his fancy. It was fast and it was a bomber. He loved the thought of owning one. He envisioned the fun he could have flying it.

Steve's commercial airline flight landed on time on the single runway airport nestled in a cove of towering mountains. The airport was surrounded on three sides with a majestic view of those mountains. The only runway pointed out over the lake. Steve caught a glimpse of the shimmering water out of the left side of the aircraft as it turned in on final approach for landing.

After landing, Steve entered the two-story terminal and was met by a man with a balding scalp and a firm handshake. His name was George Masters.

George was a retired military man and an avid aircraft collector. He specialized in old planes from past wars. He always had one or two projects in his hanger that he was tinkering with. The *Curtiss Helldiver* was his pride and joy.

Steve had a good feeling about George from their previous phone conversations regarding the aircraft ad he had placed. There was no question in Steve's mind that George understood flying and warbird aircraft. After meeting him in the Lake Tahoe Airport, his clean-cut appearance solidified Steve's original opinion of the man.

"Steve, so glad you made it on time. One can never tell with the airlines today since the 9/11 terrorist attacks. The security measures we have to put up with make a mess of travel times," George said laughingly.

"Yes it does," Steve replied. "But that's the joy of owning a charter service, it helps minimize the delays. Which brings up the question, why did I fly here commercial?"

Steve laughed and went on to explain that if he liked what he saw, he wanted to take immediate possession of George's *Helldiver* aircraft.

George had purchased the aircraft back in the mid-70s from a now defunct corporation. For many years the abandoned aircraft was stored at the Municipal Airport in Eureka, CA.

For quite a few years prior to George purchasing the aircraft, the storage charges were paid in cash for the upcoming year. An envelope would mysteriously arrive every year on the 5th of January. No other explanation would be given except a note saying the money was for storage for the upcoming year.

In 1976 the cash envelope never arrived. The airport had no owner contact information and the aircraft identification *N* number was unregistered. After six months of non-payment, the airport put the aircraft up for auction.

The plane itself was not in bad shape. Although dirty and dusty, it looked like it could fly. It appeared whoever flew it last landed the plane and just walked away. The bomb bay doors were left open for years. Various rodents and birds made it their nesting place.

George was the winning bidder. Although the plane appeared as though it could fly, George was not taking any chances. He had the plane disassembled for transportation back to his hanger at the Lake Tahoe Airport. It was a good thing George did not try to fly the plane. During the disassembly procedure, several holes in the oil cooler were discovered. It would have been disastrous to have started the engine.

Once George got the plane to Lake Tahoe, it sat in the disassembled state for several more years unattended. It was not until 1981 that George actually started the restoration process. The investment of time and money in the project was tremendous but if Steve decided to purchase the aircraft for the agreed price, it would turn George a handsome profit.

That night over dinner at one of the local casinos, Steve poured over the aircraft restoration and maintenance records. He was determined to make sure all was in order. Even though Steve's bank account showed a good number of zero's before the decimal point, he wasn't about to be frivolous.

The two men parted company that evening agreeing to meet at the airport the following morning at 10:00 a.m. Once there, Steve would take the *Helldiver* for a check ride.

Lake Tahoe Airport, California
Friday - 9:30 a.m. (PST)

The taxi dropped Steve at the front entrance of the airport terminal at 9:30 a.m. the next morning. The summer season was waning and the fall air was being ushered in on a gentle wind. The view around the airport was awe-inspiring. Steve was anxious to get in the air to capture even more of the mornings beauty.

Steve entered the general aviation tarmac after going through the usual security checks. Getting through the checkpoints was relatively easy. The non-commercial segment of the aviation industry is not as regulated as the commercial side. Even though a small plane could still pack a wallop should a terrorist desire, the emphasis on security landed on the commercial side.

George already had the canopy open as Steve walked up to the plane.

"Hey George, great day for flying, wouldn't you say?" Steve blurted.

"It's a gorgeous day. You should have a phenomenal view from up top."

George was looking down from the ladder he had propped up to the engine and told Steve, "Oil and fuel are fine. You're all set to take it for a spin."

Steve slipped into his flight suit he had carried with him. He made his usual outside pre-flight exterior inspection. He enjoyed the sleek lines of the plane. He let his hand glide over the fuselage as if petting a horse. Steve had flown some great aircrafts in his time but there just was not a comparison to this, a restored vintage warplane.

Steve climbed the ladder into the plane. Adrenaline pumped throughout his body as he settled into the cockpit. He loved flying military aircraft even though this particular aircraft was retired from active duty years earlier.

Steve nestled into the seat, buckled himself in and began studying his little flying cocoon. The cockpit gave off a steel, oily smell. The sparsely padded military aircraft seat was much less comfortable compared to the plush cloth interior his usual charter aircraft had.

Steve looked out over the aircraft's nose cowling as he watched the four bladed prop begin to spin. Soon it would bite enough air so that the rest of the aircraft would bow to its pressure and begin to move effortlessly.

Steve inched the plane forward and onto the taxiway. The eyes of many passengers in the terminal waiting for their commercial flight were glued to the *Helldiver* as Steve moved the aircraft closer to the runway for takeoff. This was a plane of unusual appearance in comparison to the present day aircraft that most people were accustomed to seeing.

Steve stopped the plane short of the departure runway to complete the final mandatory run-up before takeoff. It was during this time Steve noticed the initials *ST MPLS 62* crudely etched in the lower right corner of the instrument panel. He thought it was rather odd that with all the work George put in the plane that he would not have buffed that out. Steve made a mental note to ask George about it when he landed.

After receiving clearance for take-off, Steve moved the aircraft to the departure runway. Steve released the brakes and pushed the throttle to the firewall. The plane responded by snapping to life. It glided down the runway with the engine giving an angry roar that pierced the tranquil mountain setting. Steve pulled back on the control yoke shooting the plane skyward and tearing it loose from the gravity that held it to the ground.

The water of Lake Tahoe glistened with a turquoise blue appearance as Steve looked down from the canopy of the *1943 Curtiss SB2C Helldiver* warplane. At 2,000 feet and 275 miles per hour, the aircraft's powerful engine pummeled the valley below with a shock wave of irritating sound.

The paint scheme, flat black with silver painted leading edges, could be seen diving, climbing, and rolling from side to side, as Steve tested the aircrafts limits. Steve liked the feel of the aircraft and was sure he would purchase the plane from the balding man for the price he was asking.

For the next hour or so, Steve tested the planes agility. He imagined what the war pilot saw out of the same canopy that he was now peering through. Questions about the plane's past flooded his mind.

How many people did this plane kill? Where is the original pilot? What about the war time workers that built the plane? Is it possible any are still alive?

Due to some extraordinary events in Steve's life, he had a newfound appreciation for things of the past.

Steve was convinced he wanted this plane. He would pay George his asking price. The price was fair and with all the work George put into the restoration project…well he deserved to make a profit.

Steve turned the plane back toward the direction of the Lake Tahoe Airport. He made a gentle left turn to line up on a final approach on Runway 18 to the airport. He slowed the aircraft to landing speed. The cars below were zipping back and forth on the four-lane highway separating the lake from the airport. There was quite a bit of traffic going in and out of the casino city that morning.

However, this was a Saturday and that alone brought a terrific amount of traffic from the Sacramento, California area.

Getting set for final landing, Steve reached for the switch to extend full flaps. Almost instantly, as he flipped the switch, a piercing white light exploded around him. The light was so intense he instinctively covered his eyes with his forearm. Not only was the light unbearable but an excruciating high pitch squeal invaded Steve's inner ear. He screamed in pain. He had no idea what was happening.

Steve tried to reach for the radio but he could not seem to grasp it. The radio-mic had fallen out of its holster.

By now the thoughts of crashing again terrified him. The exploding light blinded him temporarily. All reason seemed to evacuate his mind.

Steve was determined it was not going to end this way. He slammed the throttle forward and pulled back hard on the yoke. No response. The plane continued on its descending final approach.

Steve rubbed his eyes trying to get the blood flowing back into the eye sockets so he could see to land the plane. It worked. Blurred at first, but his vision began to return.

Once his eyes could focus, he glared at the instrument panel. His mind raced in several directions. He demised that the blinding light had to be a result of something disintegrating in the cockpit. But all seemed normal.

"Something has to have failed!" He said to himself.

After a moment, Steve looked up to find the runway again. Shock overtook him at what he saw in front of him. He could see the runway okay, but gone was the terminal building. Gone was the four-lane highway. Gone was the traffic. The landscape looked entirely different.

Steve tried pulling back on the yoke to go around and take a second look but the plane would not respond. It continued landing as if it were doing it without Steve piloting the plane. He had no control of the plane. It was landing on its own!

Steve crossed where the four-lane highway should have been. It was now only a narrow two-lane road. The pavement was gray and cracking. He could see a feeble attempt had been made to fill the cracks with tar. The few cars he saw were of 1940 and 1950 vintage style sedans.

The landing gear gently kissed the runway and the aircraft rolled to a silent stop. Steve sat in stunned silence. Everything had changed. Buildings, cars, and people were fewer. George was nowhere to be seen.

Steve thought to himself, *where am I?*

CHAPTER 3

Cal Neva Casino - One Week Earlier
Thursday 8:00 p.m. (PST) - 1962

The meeting of the bosses was scheduled to take place on Thursday evening at 9:00 p.m. that day back in 1962. It was a private meeting and the arrival of each member took place secretly via commercial airline. The arrivals were spaced out over the previous several days so as not to attract attention. There was an important decision to be made, one that would make or break careers.

The attendees Antonio, Pauley, Giovanni, Lou, and Sammy enjoyed the amenities of the Cal Neva Casino. Jake, who ran the West Coast operation, was a gracious host. Although the meeting was important, that did not stop the gambling, booze, and women, which were in abundance.

Antonio and Giovanni were from the New York and New Jersey Districts. Their operation provided much of the cash that ran the entire East Coast network. Transportation and waste management was big business in the area due to the swelling population. They ran a very tight operation that had an extensive array of people answering to them.

Lou hailed from the Washington DC District. He kept a low profile by running a number of Italian restaurants in and around the area. The restaurants provided a good connection with the politicians that frequented his establishments. Of course, many of the meals were no charge...*compliments of the management.*

Pauley headed up the Pennsylvania and Ohio Districts. He kept busy with the Unions that ran strong in the area. Steel was in great demand due to the booming building business and the ironworkers contributed greatly to Pauley's authority. In addition, Pauley was a big man. No one messed with him.

Sammy came from the Florida area. Retirement properties were starting to go at a premium and construction was good. Much of the coastal areas harbored big cash spenders. Sammy had a knack of siphoning retirement accounts with the blessing of the owners. He was a terrific sales person with an enforcement posse backing him.

The members started arriving at the private dining area located behind the kitchen. The aroma of pasta filled the air. The smiles that normally greeted one another were missing. Tension replaced the smiles. They knew the business they were there to accomplish was a huge step for all of them.

Lou spoke first. "Gentlemen, as you know I was the first to raise this issue so I'll open this meeting. As I told all of you, we have a problem. Our people on the inside are feeding us some disturbing information that could damage us all. People on the Hill are starting to get loose lips and bold with their statements and plans. No question where it's coming from. It starts at the top, gentlemen, and I'm talking the very top."

Pauley was the next to speak.

"I have to agree. Lately, the Unions have been faced with some very intense audits and you all know we agreed that would not happen. Who do they think they are?"

Sammy joined in with Pauley's intensity.

"Yeah, and the tax incentives for building are in jeopardy on the South Coast. We cannot let that happen. What do they think they're doing? It would kill what we got going down there. Not only would it kill it, but if it continues it may just stop everything we got going on period."

All began mumbling amongst themselves about the troubles they were having. Each had arrived at the same conclusion, the top must be cutoff so growth down below could begin to flourish once more. Not one of them was exempt from the effects of the ongoing pressure put on the mob from the politicians. That pressure had to stop and stop quickly.

Giovanni, who most considered the powerhouse of the bunch, stood up. He picked up a glass of wine as he spoke.

"Gentlemen, gentlemen…let's stop the rumblings. No doubt, we have a problem…a problem that did not exist before the election. It can only get worse from here. All it would take is one bozo to start covering his own rear-end and from there it would all run downhill and topple us all. You all have heard my plan and yeah it's gutsy, but what are we going to do? I see no other option. So Sammy, you still got your connection to South Africa, right?"

"Of course Giovanni…stronger than ever."

"Jake, you still got connections to the Russians?" Giovanni asked.

"You bet," Jake responded.

He continued with the questioning, “Lou, can you still get us those travel plans?”

“Well it’s pretty well guarded but I have some contacts that can get it done,” he answered.

Giovanni turned to Pauley and questioned, “You can line up the pilot and plane for Jake, right?”

“You know it boss. Got ‘em all picked out and the bird too. It’s going to be a piece of cake to get him to make the trip.”

Giovanni lifted his glass of wine, paused, and said, “Sounds like we can do this and do it well. Now if we’re all in agreement to go forward with our plan, let’s raise our glasses in a toast to reclaiming our positions.”

All agreed. Glasses were raised and the operation was officially started that evening in the back room of the Cal Neva Casino.

The smiles returned to the men. They had a plan to take care of business. The pasta and wine flowed freely for the rest of the evening. Deep down each questioned whether they were taking the right path. They were undertaking the biggest move of their lives.

Lake Tahoe Airport, California - One Week Later
Friday 1:00 p.m. (PST) - 1962

What had happened? Why was everything different?’

Steve was dumbfounded.

Once again, he seemed to be in a different dimension. It had happened again! Steve was mysteriously transferred back in time but this time the plane came with him. He had no answers. No explanations. All he felt was a sinking feeling in his stomach.

Steve saw a lone man wearing a dark fedora and a gray overcoat approaching from outside a small gate that separated the parking from the tarmac. He was walking towards Steve and the *Curtiss Helldiver* airplane. Steve slowly slid the canopy open. The air smelled crisp and clean.

Looking up at Steve in the cockpit the man sarcastically said, "Well ace, you did it this time didn't you?"

"What? What did I do?" Steve inquisitively asked.

"Never mind. They told me you were a little short on brains. Get out of the stinking plane and let's go. The boss is waiting and he's not happy."

Steve was unsure what was happening. No wonder the man in the fedora thought he was stupid. Steve was dazed and confused as to his whereabouts. Suddenly Steve's world had taken a turn in time again.

Steve instinctively climbed from the plane but in a haze of uncertainty. He followed the man as instructed to a car waiting just past the airport fence. He had no idea why or where he was going.

Steve's head was still ringing from the intense moments in the cockpit. His eyes hurt and his head throbbed like a beating drum but that was secondary to his thoughts about the strange place he had landed. Nothing looked the same as it did when he took off in what he thought was just an hour or so ago.

Steve was led to a 1961 Chevy Impala Coupe that was in pristine condition. Steve entered the passenger side and followed the man with his eyes as he got in on the driver's side. As he climbed in the car, his coat slid open. Steve noticed the pistol strapped to the side of his upper chest. Steve was even more startled.

The driver started the car, placed it in gear, and stepped on the accelerator. The tires spit gravel as the Chevy sped out of the parking lot.

"Can I ask where we're going?" Steve questioned the man.

The man retaliated, "As if you don't know?"

"Listen, I'm a bit confused. All I want to know is where we are going?" Steve quipped.

"Peanut brain, where is it we're supposed to go? Does maybe the name Cal Neva sound familiar?"

The man was getting irritated with Steve's questioning.

Steve sat in silence. Whatever had happened was not right. He could tell he was in a bad situation once again. There was no telling how this all could have happened.

As the car sped to God knows where, the AM radio played an Elvis Presley song in the background. Neither man spoke to the other.

Steve picked up a newspaper lying on the front seat. The headline read *Massive Storm Approaches West Coast.* What shocked Steve the most was the date on the newspaper. It read *October 11, 1962.*

It had happened again. It appeared Steve was transformed into another time era. He was trying to process in his mind all that had happened. It was too much. His mind drifted off into his memory to a faraway place in the past.

This same sort of thing had happened before. He had experienced the teleportation to a different era. The outcome was almost too much to understand. How and where was this going? Soon the Elvis Presley song faded as Steve's thoughts turned further inward to another time and place.

His mind brought him to a place long in the past where he seemed to build a life far from home. A life that was simple and carefree, that somehow had taken him to a place in the 1860's.

He thought of Jean, the woman he had fallen in love with and lost. Lost because he abruptly returned to the present day and left a life that took place better than 100 years in the past.

Steve was jostled from his thoughts when the Chevy rocked side to side as it pulled to the front of the Cal Neva Casino. Steve was amazed at what he was seeing. The cars, the way people dressed, the building itself all testified that Steve was far from the present he had known.

Almost as quickly as the car stopped, the passenger door opened. A rough looking individual had opened the door and had his huge hand wrapped around Steve's upper arm. He pulled Steve from the car with a jerk. It was useless to fight against him because of the man's size and strength. Steve could smell the musty aroma of a half eaten cigar sticking out from the man's lips.

"Hey, easy big fella!" Steve exclaimed with a bit of sarcasm in his voice. "Let's be civil here. I can walk you know."

The big man just grunted as he pulled Steve through the casino doors and trudged through the gaming floor. They passed a handful of what seemed to be locals sitting at slot machines methodically dropping nickels into the non-electronic machines. No one took notice, or cared to take notice, as the big man pulled Steve into a hallway that led to a private room at the back of the main floor.

Steve recognized the era. The cars, the clothes, the people…it all testified that he was in 1962. In his thoughts he questioned, *had it really happened again or was he dreaming?'*

Steve wondered how he could have been transported to another time era like before. Too many things seemed strangely out of place. He still had no clue how it started and why. Nevertheless, it felt as real as flying the *Helldiver* aircraft just a short time before. The man's grip made it all seem so real.

The thug pulled Steve through the long hallway and into a room that already had the door open. The room was dark except for a wooden chair positioned under a bright light. Smoke filtered through the rays of light like mist on a foggy morning.

The man that pulled Steve from the car released his grip and pushed him into the wooden chair. As Steve's eyes became a bit more accustomed to the room light, he saw a few men lurking in the corners on 1960's style furniture.

A man wearing a white fedora, pin stripped suit, and white spats emerged from the darkened corner of the room. He was a large man. He was easily six foot four and had the build to match. As he spoke, his voice was slow, distinct, and rather raspy.

"Your instructions were to have that bird here yesterday. Samantha and her crew had the boat in place ready for the drop. But you didn't show. Do you know how much explaining I had to do? Do you have any idea the predicament this has put me in?"

By the sound of the man's voice Steve could tell he was extremely agitated. He spoke in a condescending tone. Steve realized the situation he was in was not good. He had to explain to them that they had the wrong man.

"Hold on just a minute--."

Before Steve could finish, the man lashed out with his left hand and smashed it into the side of Steve's face. Blood trickled from his lip. Steve wiped the blood on his sleeve as the big man lashed out with a verbal attack.

"Shut up! I don't want to hear any of your idiotic excuses. You messed up somewhere along the line and I ought to take you out back and take your head off. I can't believe I have to let you live because no one, but no one, ever crosses Jake and survives the ordeal! But... as circumstances have it you're the only one that can fly that bird and drop the goods precisely where we need it."

Steve was extremely confused...confused because once again he was caught in a time warp. He tried to comprehend the situation but it was just too bizarre to make anything of it just yet.

The man stood for a moment and gave Steve a stare. Neither spoke. After a few tense moments of each man intently sizing up the other, the big man looked away. He motioned to another person standing in the corner. Undoubtedly, this was one of the big man's bodyguards.

The two men whispered softly and in low tones. Steve could only make out a few words here and there. However, one of the words stood out in a chilling manner. He heard Jake, who seemed to be in charge, say the words "kill him."

Steve now knew emphatically that he was not in a good situation. Just as he had done previously when he found himself in the late 1860's, he knew he was going to have to think and act quickly to spare his life.

Jake returned to Steve. He moved his face within six inches of Steve's. He felt the breath of the big man on his face. His breath smelled of bad booze. His eyes burned with a steel blue intensity. They were filled with rage. The big man just grunted, smirked, and walked away. Steve had to do something and do it now.

"Wait!" he blurted. "I know I let you down but after I got here to Tahoe…I was confused on the instructions after that."

Steve remembered Jake had said something about dropping something so he started to bluff.

"I knew the drop had to be precise so rather than screw it up I came here to get directions and instructions one more time."

The big man paused and sighed without facing Steve. He rubbed his face with his hand, turned and blurted, "Then why are you one day late?"

Steve stuttered, "I . . . must of . . . uh . . . I didn't…"

Before Steve could finish his sentence, Jake screamed at him.

"I've already told you once I don't want to hear your excuses!"

He moved in close on Steve's face.

"I can't believe what I am about to say."

Jake turned and whispered something to two men in the room standing close by. Both nodded at the instructions and left the room. Jake continued with Steve.

"As I said, I can't believe I have to give you one more chance but I have no choice. You're the only one that can make the precise nighttime drop without causing suspicion. Here are your instructions one more time and I suggest you not forget them again.

"Fly that bird to the Eureka Municipal Airport off the Northern California coast. At precisely 11:30 p.m., make a low-level pass down Runway 34 at 100 feet. When the runway reaches the end, climb to 2,000 feet, and circle the airport until you see a flare. Turn and follow the coast south.

"In approximately 15 minutes, you will see a rock formation jutting out of the water about 100 feet tall and about 1,000 yards off the coast. This is called Sugarloaf Island. On shore to your left will be The Cape Mendocino Lighthouse. Fly at 200 feet between the two and as close to Sugarloaf Island as possible. Drop the box precisely at the base of the rock formation as you fly by. Have you got that?"

Jake was sarcastic with his question. Steve responded with the same sarcasm.

"Yeah, I've got it. But where is this box I'm supposed to drop?" Steve asked.

Just then the door opened and the two muscle men returned carrying a wooden crate. It looked strangely familiar to Steve. He was stunned to see it was the same crate that was delivered to his office weeks earlier!

The two men were setting it on the floor when one of them stumbled and the crate came crashing down. The lid popped off and a couple of gold bars fell to the floor from within the crate.

Both men looked at each other as if trying to blame someone. Jake on the other hand was furious. Without hesitation, he pulled a gun from under his jacket and shot both men dead on the spot. Calmly, he returned the gun to the inside of his suit coat and said, "Two less I have to worry about stealing from me."

Steve was astonished at the turn of events. He could hardly believe he just saw two people killed in cold blood.

Next, he could not believe the crate of gold. But it was not the gold that astonished him…it was the crate! It was the same one he was carrying when he crashed his Cessna 310 aircraft several weeks earlier, the same wooden crate that turned up empty. He questioned whether the crate was originally filled with gold.

The turn of events was overwhelming. Here he was seemingly 40 some years in the past and once again, he is faced with flying the same crate.

"Now listen," Jake sarcastically stated, "you see this crate . . . well that gold in that crate you have mistakenly seen is very important to me. Unfortunately for you is the temptation to fly off with my gold. Nevertheless, as you see I have very little patience for mistakes in judgment. The less people know the contents of that crate, the better.

"I'm a man with many connections and my tracks are well covered. If you get brave, greedy, or even breathe wrong and try to run with my gold, I will know it and believe me, I will deal with you harshly. Do we have an understanding here?"

"Uh, yeah," Steve responded.

Deep down his heart was pounding and his brain was on overload. This was a life or death predicament.

"Billy, get in here!" Jake yelled.

A thin tall man walked in the room. He wore a tan suit, wire framed round glasses and a brown fedora that almost covered his ears. He had the appearance of an accountant rather than an individual who was associated with such a band of thugs.

"Billy, remember what your instructions were?" Jake asked.

Billy answered with a sinister sounding voice, "You bet, and there won't be any screw ups."

Steve could now see the intense eyes of the man. He thought to himself, *this is no accountant.*

Without as much as a nod to anyone in the room, Jake headed for the exit. He just simply growled instructions.

"Get this room cleaned up."

A couple of men came in and began removing the bodies of the two dead men.

Steve thought to himself, "What kind of crowd is this to have two men shot without as much as an inquiry by anyone?"

Billy walked to Steve sitting in the chair. He circled as he lit a cigarette. He leaned his head into within a foot of Steve's face and blew a smoke ring.

"You and me Stevie boy...we're going to be this close. So close," Billy clinched his index and thumb together in front of Steve's face, "you're not going to even be able to spit. You got that?"

Steve swallowed hard, "Yeah, I think I get the picture."

Billy snapped his fingers and two men came in with a two-wheeler and scooped up the crate of gold.

"You know what to do with that. Get it done."

"We're on our way Billy," the larger man said.

Billy turned to Steve and simply said, "Let's go."

Billy, Steve, and a third man walked out of the dimly lit office and into the casino gaming area. The sparse crowd of gamblers never looked up. It was if they knew there was trouble but knew better than to get involved or ask questions.

Billy pushed Steve towards the front door of the casino. As they exited the building, a black 1958 Lincoln Continental screeched to a halt. The back door flung open and Billy pushed Steve into the car. He tossed the half-lit cigarette to the curb and slid in after Steve.

The slamming of the doors startled Steve. The two men rode in silence in the back seat as the driver drove off.

Steve's mind had so many questions. *Why had this happened? Who were these street thugs? What about that crate?*

The questions kept repeating themselves in Steve's mind while Billy calmly smoked another cigarette.

CHAPTER 4

Lake Tahoe Airport, California
Friday 1:12 p.m. (PST) - 1962

Marty and Tony drove to the airport with the crate of gold as instructed by Billy. They pulled up to the *Helldiver* Steve had just parked.

"Tony, are you sure you can rig this thing to blow tonight at 11:52 p.m. sharp?" Marty asked.

Marty was a stout man. He was always looking over his shoulder. He always worked under pressure. The pressure was not caused by his duties but rather by his nervous nature. He constantly worried about everything.

Tony looked at Marty not believing he was questioning his expertise in munitions.

"Marty, quit worrying. You're gonna kill yourself with all this worry. Of course it will be rigged for 11:52 p.m. That's the plan and I plan on delivering."

Tony was quite emphatic with his answer. He had his own pressure and he did not need Marty adding to it.

Tony exited the car and climbed beneath the plane. He reached up and released the safety latch for the aerial bomb compartment. Next, he climbed to the plane's cockpit, reached in and released the bomb bay doors. They swung open on cue.

Tony climbed from the cockpit and underneath the plane. With a flashlight in hand, he examined the best area to place the explosives. He determined directly up and behind the mechanism that operated the bay doors was best. It was out of the way of the doors opening and the blast was sure to rip the fuselage apart without any hindrance.

He retrieved his tools from the trunk and began fashioning a platform to hold the explosive charge. Once satisfied the unit would hold, he gently lifted the explosives from the trunk. Beads of sweat could be seen on his brow as he carefully secured the explosives to the platform.

Next, he secured the trigger mechanism to the bomb bay doors. The trigger was rigged so when the doors were opened it would make the bomb hot and two minutes later it would explode, sending shrapnel throughout the fuselage, and ripping the plane to pieces.

Marty did not watch Tony as he rigged the explosives. He was busy preparing the wooden crate for the drop. He had fashioned a low-level parachute to the top of the crate and a raft to the bottom. As the crate was dropped from the plane, a ripcord would open the parachute and the chute would trigger the raft inflation valve. This would allow the crate to land in the water upright and floating.

Tony completed his work and dropped from the belly of the plane. It was now time to place the crate of gold in the bomb compartment of the plane. However, they realized it was much too heavy for them to lift and secure it in place on board the plane.

Tony commented, "I don't like it, but we're going to have to unload this thing and then reload it in the plane once we have the box rigged to the bombing mechanism."

Marty just sighed. The thought of unloading and reloading a box full of gold bars in broad daylight added to the nervousness he already had.

Tony opened the trunk and removed the lid to the crate of gold. The two men unloaded the bars of gold out of the crate and placed them in the trunk for the time being.

Once completed, Tony re-entered the bomb compartment of the plane. Marty picked the empty crate from the trunk and held it in place in the bomb compartment area while Tony attached it to the plane's bomb release apparatus. After it was secure, Marty backed the car as close to the plane as possible to help eliminate any prying eyes.

Tony moved to position himself in the plane's bomb compartment so he was above the open crate. Marty began handing Tony the gold bars from the trunk. Tony placed each one carefully in the crate.

Both men broke into a cold sweat while completing this task. The sweat was not from the strenuous work but from having that much gold so close.

The two men worked in silence with the one exception. It was a comment made by Marty. He stopped momentarily and looked at Tony. Tony was not sure if he saw greed or fear in the big man's eyes.

Marty simply stated, "When they say gold fever...I can really understand."

The two men finished their task of transferring the gold back into the crate. Tony then placed four steel bands around the crate and placed a rather large lock on the bands, locking them all in place. Although the parachute and raft were going to work, they did not want the crate crashing open and spilling its contents should the parachute or raft fail.

Tony dropped down from the bomb compartment, dusted his hands off and climbed to the cockpit once more. He gingerly closed the bomb bay doors. Marty nervously watched. He did not want the explosives going off prematurely. The plane was now rigged with explosives and the crate of gold was rigged for the drop as planned.

Tony left the airport confident in the job he had done. Marty left with a bad case of nerves.

The Motel Room
Friday 2:05 p.m. (PST) - 1962

The big Lincoln pulled up to a neon sign that simply read *Motel.* Underneath the larger sign, a smaller white sign swayed in the breeze that read *Vacancy.* There were no cars in the parking lot. The driver bypassed the office and stopped in front of the room at the end of the building. He turned the car off. It was eerily silent.

Billy told Steve, “Come on, get out.”

He led Steve to the motel room with a dimly lit light inside. A single insect buzzed repeatedly around a bug zapper a few yards from the room as Billy fumbled with the doorknob. He then pushed Steve through the open door.

“Sit down over there!” he barked at Steve.

Steve headed to the lone chair stuck in the corner of the room. He was getting a bit irritated with his situation. As he passed the bed, he noticed the bedspread had been wrinkled as if someone had been lying on it already.

Billy motioned to the driver. He whispered to him and then pulled a few bills from his pocket. Steve could not hear the conversation. The driver acknowledged Billy's words and left. Steve heard the car engine roar to life and then speed off.

Billy stretched out on the bed and propped himself up on his left elbow. He looked at Steve through his glasses as if studying him. He removed his fedora revealing a huge jagged scar just below his hairline. His hair, matted and graying, only sparsely covered his balding scalp.

Billy finally spoke after a few moments.

"You have a confused look on your face."

Steve, not sure on how to answer, sarcastically said, "Oh really."

Billy chuckled and then stopped abruptly.

"Jake gives no room for error you know. Just do what you're told and things will be just fine. Lose your way...well, let's just say it wouldn't end pretty."

Steve realized he had to find a way to get information from this guy. He had no clue as to what this was all about. However, deep down he sensed there was a web of people involved. There seemed to be much more to this than what Steve had seen thus far.

After a few minutes of silence, Billy rose from the bed and moved to a wooden table and chair opposite of Steve. He lit another cigarette and started playing with a deck of well-used cards that were lying on the table.

Steve spoke up first, "Say Billy, where you from?"

"Now why would you want to know that?" Billy sarcastically answered without looking up from his cards.

"You said we're going to be that close."

Steve mimicked Billy's earlier hand motions.

"I thought I should know who you are if we're going to be stuck here for a little while."

Billy just chuckled and simply said slowly, "Right."

The two men sat in silence. Billy calmly played Solitaire while Steve nervously sat in the chair across the room trying to get a grasp on what was happening, and more importantly, why.

A sharp knock on the door startled Steve back to reality. Billy went to the door, pulled a gun from his waistband and with his back to the doorframe yelled out, "Yeah, who is it?"

"It's me...Marty. Open up."

Billy positioned his gun back in his waistband and said, "Hold on a minute."

Billy moved to the window and with a quick yank of the drawstring on the window shade, it let loose with a snap. Billy approached the chair where Steve was.

"Put your arms behind you."

Steve did as he was instructed. Billy tied Steve's hands and arms behind him.

"There, that should keep you put for awhile. I need to take care of business outside. Don't try anything foolish. I'm sure you know it would be the last thing you would do."

Billy moved to the motel door, unbolted the lock, and cautiously opened the door. He quickly glanced around outside before stepping out and closing it behind him.

Steve sat in silence surveying the room for an escape route. It was futile. There was no way out other than a bathroom window but he could see it would make too much racket to open. Besides, Billy had tied the shade drawstring tightly around his wrists. The multiple wraps made it too difficult to break.

Steve could hear the two men talking outside the motel. Marty spoke first.

"Billy, I don't know about this plan. If this goes bad we're looking at a mighty long time in the slammer."

"I know, I know, I know," Billy responded.

Steve could sense a bit of apprehension in Marty's voice. Billy tried to ease Marty's tension.

"The New York boys called this one and you know Jake does what they tell him. They all agreed to it."

Marty lit a cigarette and handed one to Billy. Billy tossed the butt of the one he had been smoking in the parking lot and started smoking the one Marty offered.

Marty's voice had a crescendo to it as he spoke.

"This isn't a simple hit like the others. This is major. We will have the entire U.S. Government investigating this. If you ask me, there are just too many players involved in this one. Way too many players! I mean come on, you got the East Coast directing the West Coast, the West Coast using their connections with the Russians, you got the Russians contracting the hit, we got this gold to finance the deal…"

"Marty! Marty! Cool it! You're working yourself into a huge frenzy. Yeah, we got alot of players but who do you think the government would go after if something goes wrong?"

"Well duh Billy…us!" Marty emphatically answered.

"No Marty you got it all wrong. Who were the main players in getting JFK elected? The public thinks it was them but you and I both know it was our organization. The bosses got him elected not the people. The government is not stupid. They know it was us. They also know the Russians have been looking for a piece of this administration with that Cuban missile fiasco that took place.

"Lately with all the whoring around the White House has been doing, the boys in New York are afraid of exposed connections and leaks. They figure with taking out the President it will stop any compromise. Don't you see...the first ones they'll go after are the Russians?"

Marty retorted, "Yeah but why pay for the hit in gold? If you ask me, it's too hard to handle and creates too much exposure. Cold hard cash is much easier to handle than having this yo-yo drop gold from a plane."

"Marty, are you stupid or what? If we're taking out JFK, why would we finance it with his currency? That leaves too much of a trail. You pay in gold and after that it can be melted down into some bimbo's earrings, completely untraceable."

"Yeah, I suppose you're right Billy. I'm just so blasted nervous. I still say too many players. Too many things to go wrong. I hope we can keep it together.

"Anyway Billy, I just stopped by to tell you the bomb and the gold are in place. Two minutes after the 11:50 p.m. drop at the island, that plane goes up in a big bang. Tony not only has it rigged to blow after the drop but our guys can blow it from the ground on command for our protection.

"Regardless, two minutes after those bomb doors are opened, that plane is toast. That pilot has no chance of hitting the water alive. That bird will be in so many pieces you won't be able to tell the pilot from fish guts.

"Listen Billy, you gotta make sure that drop takes place on time. Do you hear me? On time. If he's late, kaboom! We lose the gold and any chance of staying alive. You got that Billy…two minutes."

Billy responded with irritation, "Yeah I got it. Quit worrying! This guy will drop on time. Okay? Don't worry. We got this."

Marty just nodded without saying a word. However, his facial expressions said he was not buying it.

"Listen, I'll let Jake know you are on your way to check in. Hey, how's Lily and the kids?" Billy asked.

He wanted to change the subject and settle Marty down a bit.

"Just great," Marty responded.

"Martha is in her very first school play the day after tomorrow. Lily and I both plan on being there for that. So yeah, the family is doing good, really good. Thanks for asking. Catch you later."

"Ok Marty, kiss Lily and the kids for me. See you tomorrow."

Steve was dumbfounded. Assassinate JFK! Did his ears hear right? He somehow managed to land in the middle of the biggest murder the world has ever seen. Questions would circulate for years of what really surrounded the JFK assassination in Dallas.

He wondered if he could somehow change the course of history by foiling this plot. However, was he going to come out alive? Talk of a bomb on his plane scared him. His life was scheduled to end today at 11:52 p.m. if he did not do something. He only had minimal time to figure it out.

Steve somehow had to thwart the plans of the gold drop. The thought of saving JFK and his own life was immersed in uncertainty. He had no clue as of yet how he would accomplish this feat.

Billy came back in the motel room and bolted the door behind him. He marched straight to the nightstand and dialed a number on the rotary phone.

After a moment, the other party answered.

"Hey Jake its Billy. I think we got a problem with Marty. He's got a case of the jimmies."

Billy paused while listening to Jake on the other end of the phone.

He answered to Jake's comments, "Yeah, I think you're right. It has to be done. We can't afford any loose lips on this one."

Again, Billy paused while Jake spoke.

Billy responded, "Yep, on his way right now. Poor Lily, but she knew what she married into. I'll make sure she's taken care of. We're good here. Later."

Billy hung up the phone, walked to Steve, and untied him. "Gotta make sure we get blood to those arms because you've got a big flight later tonight."

Billy had no idea Steve had heard the entire conversation and plan. Steve's military training screamed at him…the element of surprise! However, no one was more surprised than Steve was at this moment.

CHAPTER 5

Cal Neva Casino
Friday, 4:12 p.m. (PST) - 1962

Marty pulled into the rear of the Cal Neva Casino. He parked near the private entrance to Jake's suite. He turned the car off and paused momentarily. He breathed a heavy sigh. The pressures of the last couple of days had taken a toll on him. He still had a nervous feeling in the pit of his stomach about their assassination plans.

Marty was led into the private room by the bodyguard at the door. Marty had no clue what he faced concerning Jake. He always had a nervous feeling whenever meeting with him. He had seen the ruthlessness of Jake and inwardly he never trusted him.

Jake greeted Marty with an awkward smile.

Marty spoke first, "Hey Jake. Hope I'm not intruding."

Jake was sitting on the couch with three beautiful women surrounding him. He reached into his pocket, pulled out a roll of hundred dollar bills, peeled off several of them, and handed them to the women.

"Go enjoy the casino girls," he told them.

They giggled, said their thanks, and rushed off to the casino eager to spend their new found cash.

Jake meticulously rose from the couch. He strolled to the window and leaned against the frame with his left arm while resting his right hand on his hip.

He stared out the window as he asked, "Well Marty, all set with the bird?"

"Yes sir. At 11:52 that plane will be blown to a millions of pieces and none bigger than a Cal Neva silver dollar."

Marty was trying to hide the nervousness he felt. He tried to project confidence in his speech to Jake.

Jake turned from the window and faced Marty, "Good Marty. Good. Like a drink?"

Marty declined, "No thanks. I have to get home to the wife. She's making my favorite dish tonight, ravioli with Italian sausage. She's a great cook."

"Hmmm, sounds really good. I'll have to try that sometime. Listen Marty…I think you'll have to eat the leftovers this time."

Jake spoke with authority to Marty.

"You know Marty, this is a big job for us, maybe the largest ever. You sure you don't want a drink?"

Marty declined again as Jake moved to the liquor cabinet and poured himself a drink.

"As I was saying…the largest ever. We need to stay off the radar until this thing blows over. I don't think it's a good thing to be seen around town for right now.

Why don't you go to the dock and stay on my boat for a few days? Frankie and Lester are headed there now. You guys go relax, enjoy yourselves, do a little fishing if you like. Okay?"

"Okay boss, you know what's best."

Jake smiled at Marty and said, "You're a good boy Marty."

Jake patted him on the cheekbone.

"A good boy."

Marty turned and walked out the door with Frankie and Lester close behind. Jake called out as the men were leaving.

"Hey Frankie, come here a minute."

Jake motioned him to come close.

Frankie whispered, "Yeah boss, what's up?"

Jake hesitated with his response. He looked over Frankie's shoulder to make sure Marty was not within hearing distance.

"Marty…he's a good boy…but a nervous boy and we can't afford to let anyone screw up this job. When you get him to the boat…make sure he sleeps with the fishes."

With a smirk, Frankie simply said, "You got it boss."

Frankie turned and followed Lester and Marty who were already out the door. The three men rode to Jake's dock on Lake Tahoe in silence. Marty's nerves were on edge and he felt uneasy going to the boat with these guys. He wasn't sure why he felt uneasy, it just was happening.

They parked the car and all three walked the pier to where Jake had his boat docked. The wooden deck creaked under the weight of the men's feet. The small fish that lingered below the pier dashed from their hiding place with each sound of the men's footsteps.

Jake had his boat parked at the end of a long pier. The vessel was large and built with all the amenities available. The men climbed aboard. Lester started the engine while Frankie untied the moorings.

The men continued in silence as they idled out of the marina and headed out to the lake.

Marty sat on the boat deck staring at the diminishing shoreline. The sun was beginning to set in the Western horizon. He thought of his wife's ravioli. He thought of his daughter's school program.

As a tear slowly crept down his cheek, the plastic bag quickly covered his head, covered his breath, and covered his thoughts. His struggle was useless against the grip of Frankie and Lester. Death came quickly. He did not even feel the icy water encase his still warm body.

The Motel Room
Friday 6:21 p.m. (PST) -1962

Steve's mind still reeled from the conversation Billy had with Marty.

He thought, "How can this be?"

Somehow he was destined to be involved with the assassination of JFK, the President of the United States! It would be a deed that would go down in the chronicles of history as the most audacious act of violence upon any U.S. President.

It was all so confusing. The only thing he was certain of was one minute he takes off flying a warbird in present time and lands back in the 1960's. His mind was racing with questions about how to get back to present time and if he would ever see his family again.

He wondered if somehow he could visit his family in Minnesota while here in the 1960's and if he did, would he see himself as a young child? What about his family? Would history be re-written again?

It was too much to comprehend. Steve thought his first order of business was to try to save JFK from being assassinated. His American heritage ran deep and if he could somehow save the President, he was darn well going to do it.

The first thing he had to do was to gather as much information from Billy as possible without raising suspicions. The sooner he could find out more about the dastardly plans of the men, the quicker he could come up with a scheme to foil the intentions of this group.

Billy continued playing cards in their motel room. His was moving slow because he was going over everything in his mind. He thought about all his associates involved with this job.

Billy thought about Marty. He first met him five years ago. They worked together on a few projects for Jake. Billy would always kid Marty for his attention to details. Everything had its place in Marty's mind. It all had to be perfect.

Billy worked his way through the ranks in Jake's organization in and around the Tahoe/Reno area. He gained the respect of Jake and his peers doing jobs no one else had the nerve to do. He had a past filled with extortion, bribery, assault and even murder. Billy had no problem leaning hard on people who did not pay and play according to Jake's rules.

Jake promoted Billy's status to that of being Jake's right hand man. Billy had collected on a huge gambling debt that one of Jake's *business associates* had racked up. When Billy returned with the money that was owed by the individual, plus a little more for good measure, Jake was quite thrilled. He was even more impressed when he learned Billy had fixed the problem for good. That individual would no longer have to worry about gambling debts or any kind of debt, not even his funeral debt.

With all the pain Billy had inflicted on others, he could not help but feel sorry for Marty's family. Marty would go on jobs with Billy and be just as ruthless as he was but at the end of the day, he could turn it off and think of his wife and kids with kindness. Marty was a family man at heart.

Billy was impressed with Marty's ability to turn off the job. He wasn't so fortunate. Billy felt his emotions were hardened far past repair by the things he had done.

Steve broke the two men's silence. "Hey Billy, can I ask you something?"

"Yeah, what is it?"

"I couldn't help notice that gold back at the Cal Neva. Where did your boss get so much gold?"

Billy looked up from his cards and stared intently at Steve.

"Listen, you saw what happened to the two guys that carried the gold in. Jake has zero tolerance for incompetence. I can't believe you got away with being one day late. So I suggest you not concern yourself with what you saw in that crate. You're getting your pay on this and that is all you should concern yourself with."

Steve never heard them mention anything about pay...just the loss of life. He was hoping to get a little more from Billy on what was going on. Steve asked again, but Billy was not budging on the information. Steve determined he was going to have to take a more direct approach.

After a few moments, Steve started questioning again but this time it was about his instructions.

"Listen Billy, Jake gave me specific instructions on what to do and when to do it. You have been no help to me in understanding my role in this. What is it you want of me?"

Billy rose to his feet, walked to the edge of the bed, and sat down facing Steve. He just stared as if he were trying to find the right words. Finally he spoke.

"Hey, I've got no beef against you. Not showing up on time is Jake's concern. To be quite frank with you, I don't care how or who gets this job done. I just want it over and precisely at 11:50 p.m. tonight when you drop that gold at the base of Sugarloaf Island…it will be over. At that point, my part in all this is done."

Steve saw his opening.

"Well that's all fine and dandy but what happens afterwards? Do I take the plane back to Eureka, fly off into the sunset, bail out…just what do you want me to do?"

Billy swallowed hard before answering. He struggled to find the right words. He had not counted on Steve asking this. In Billy's mind, it would be done when the plane with Steve in it blew up. He had to come up with a quick answer for Steve.

"Uh, you're going to…uh…going to bring the plane back to the Eureka Airport. Yeah, that's it, just bring it back for now. We'll figure out where it goes from there."

Billy's slight miscue in body language told Steve what he already knew was true. At 11:52 p.m., the plane would be blown to pieces and he along with it, if he did not do something soon.

A car was heard parking near the door. The driver that brought them to the motel had finally returned. Billy peeked out the blinds then opened the door for him. He nodded at Billy as he walked into the room. Billy acknowledged the nod and just smiled.

The driver had returned with a bag full of cheeseburgers and fries from a local diner. The bottom of the bag was covered in cooking oil but the aroma smelled wonderful. Billy reached in the bag and gave Steve one of the cheeseburgers with fries.

"Eat up," he said, "it's going to be a long night."

Steve devoured the sandwich. It was delicious. He surmised it must have tasted so good because it did not contain the preservatives present day food has. The taste was one he remembered from his childhood days.

After the three had eaten, Billy walked over and retrieved a duffle bag from the corner. He opened it and pulled out a hand held two-way radio and another electronic device that had a button switch located on the top.

He handed both to the driver and said, "Okay Luke, I want you to set up on the north side of Grass Valley at the Nevada County Air Park. I'll radio when you should be on the lookout."

Luke took both items and said, "Got it. I'll talk to you soon."

He turned and walked out the door with the items under his arm. Steve listened as the sound of the car's engine faded into the distance. He could not quite understand the significance of what he just witnessed.

Soon afterwards, a second car arrived. Frankie, with Lester standing beside him, knocked on the motel door. Once again, Billy peeked out the window checking to see who it was. Billy opened the door and greeted them with a solemn look on his face. Frankie knew what Billy was thinking.

"Listen Billy, no hard feelings about Marty. I know you and him got along pretty good but business is business and when Jake says jump, well you know we gotta. You understand don't you?"

Billy shrugged, "Yeah, I know...been there myself. Anyway, let's get this thing started."

Billy retrieved the duffel bag as he had with Luke. He handed both men a two-way radio and one of the electronic button devices from the bag.

"Lester, I want you to head to Chico and Frankie, you go on up to Redding. When you get there, park on the airport property near the runway and wait for the plane to fly by."

Billy leaned in close to the two men and whispered softly. He did not want Steve to hear.

"Uh guys..."

Billy looked back at Steve to make sure he was not in earshot.

"Keep a close eye on this bird. Any trouble or if the plane goes off course...anything, you blow it. Jake would rather lose the gold than have some two-bit pilot fly off with it. You guys understand?"

Both men nodded in agreement and then left to go to their respective locations. Frankie would drop Lester at the Chico Airport and then continue on to the Redding Airport.

Jake had taken precautions against Steve bolting with the plane and the gold. Not only was Tony to rig the plane to explode after the gold drop, but plans were put in place to detonate the bomb from the ground should Steve get an ingenious idea and fly off course.

Luke, Lester, and Frankie each had an electronic trigger mechanism that could blow the bomb in the aircraft should Steve try to make a run for it with the plane. All of them were instructed to radio in once Steve completed his fly over at the respective airports.

Jake left nothing to chance on this one. This job was far too important to mess up. He had methodically planned each step. This was going to happen tonight and nothing was going to stop him from completing the mission.

Pacific Ocean - California Coast
Friday 6:30 p.m. (PST) - 1962

Five miles off the coast of Teal Islands, California, a fishing trawler struggled to maintain its position of Latitude 40°40'32.04 N and Longitude 124°25'16.41 W. A lone red light glowed from the highest point on the boat piercing the early evening darkness.

Down below in the dimly lit galley three Russian nationals, Krill, Mikhail, and Stanislav were having a conversation. They ribbed each other on who was the strongest of the three. They also played cards and drank shots of vodka while waiting for their American contacts to show.

An American boat slipped unnoticed within a mile of the Russian ship. Don Carlo was at the helm of the American boat. Samantha, Vinnie, and Little Al stood on deck straining to see through a fog that was enveloping the ship. Samantha peered into the binoculars. She had them trained on the Russian boat.

"See anything Samantha?" Don Carlo called from the wheelhouse.

"I don't see anything except that red light. Looks like no other boats in the area. Let's give it a few more minutes. I want to make sure no one else is around when we do this."

She glanced at her watch, "We're still good on time."

Samantha was anxious for this moment. This entire ordeal was now on her shoulders. She could not fail at any cost.

Don Carlo maintained their position. Vinnie pulled his Colt 45 from his shoulder holster. He cocked a round into the chamber and returned it to his holster. Little Al repositioned his automatic weapon hidden beneath his overcoat.

Vinnie pulled the burlap bag at his feet a little closer. He was in charge of its contents. All four stood in silence as Samantha kept a watchful eye on the Russian boat.

Samantha lowered the binoculars and said, "Ok boys, we're good. Let's get this party started."

Don Carlo cranked up the boat engines, turned on the running lights, and headed for the Russian boat. The American boat looked like a freight train at sea barreling down on the Russian trawler.

Vladimir had no difficulty in spotting the American ship headed for them. He left the wheelhouse and called down to Krill in the galley.

"They are coming!"

Krill made eye contact with Mikhail and Stanislav.

In his Russian accent he said, "We are about to make history for our country and Americans."

All three smiled and made a toast. This was the night they had planned and waited for.

The American ship approached from the stern. Don Carlo gently eased the American boat next to the Russian trawler. The sea was an angry swell of white caps. The waves tossed both boats in different directions.

Stanislav tossed four large buoys overboard and tied them in place so the two boats could mate without crushing each other. Don Carlo maneuvered the American vessel closer to the Russians. Vinnie and Little Al tossed the mooring lines to the outstretched arms of Vladimir and Mikhail. Both pulled the lines tight and secured the two boats together.

Samantha led Vinnie, Little Al, and Don Carlo onto the Russian boat. Vinnie carried the burlap bag with him.

Samantha reached out to shake the hand of Krill while the others watched.

"Krill, I'm Samantha and I'm the one you've been in contact with. No need for small talk, let's get this done. We need time to get into position."

Krill was a little puzzled but said nothing. He wondered what Samantha meant by, *time to get into position.*

Samantha and Vinnie followed the three Russians down into the galley of the ship. Little Al, Don Carlo, and Vladimir stayed on deck. The three glanced warily at one another but never spoke. Each had their trigger finger cocked and ready to go should there be trouble. The three were just men in the same, but two were American and one was Russian, a combination that was at odds with each other over political beliefs.

Krill and Stanislav seated themselves at the table while Mikhail sat on a bunk against the wall. Samantha sat down across from the two while Vinnie plunked the burlap bag in the middle of the table and stayed standing.

Samantha reached in the bag and pulled out two gleaming gold bricks. They made a metallic thud as she placed them on the galley table.

Krill looked at the gold and then back at Mikhail and Stanislav. His facial expressions revealed his confusion. Krill started speaking in Russian to his comrades in an elevated tone.

Samantha quickly interjected, "Hold on. . .just hold on one minute here! We speak in English only. Do you understand?"

Tensions were obviously growing among the five below. The Russians were starting to feel betrayed. Krill finally spoke up in his Russian accent.

"Yes, we speak English for you. We have problem. Deal was twenty-five bricks. You bring two."

Samantha responded, "Yes, our deal is for twenty-five bricks but we had a slight problem with the plane we are using for our gold drop. The pilot missed his arrival deadline by a day. I don't know why, that is just what I have been told. You do understand that precautions are put in place so nothing can be traced back to this being an American hit on JFK, don't you?"

"Yes, we understand...we understand our gold is not here!" Krill said excitedly.

Mikhail stood pulling back his coat to reveal his side arm. Vinnie placed his hand near his pistol ready to draw should Mikhail make any further advances. Samantha, wanting to dismantle the growing aggression, quickly intervened.

"Come on people...let's calm down. We don't want to do anything stupid here!

"Krill, we do have twenty-five bricks on a plane at the Lake Tahoe Airport. The pilot, who had no clue what he was going to be doing, showed up one day late. We have the gold.

"Now, my contacts know this is not your problem but are willing to give you these two bricks as security. These are your two bricks to keep for yourself to compensate for the few hours of delay on our part.

"Our plane is going to fly over the Eureka Airport at exactly 11:30 p.m. tonight signaling our gold drop. We would have had him come earlier but we need the airport to be closed and that only happens after dark. You can certainly understand the cloak of secrecy we must maintain?"

Krill grunted as Mikhail started speaking excitedly in Russian. Krill held his hand up to quiet Mikhail. He looked at his comrades as if he could read their minds.

"So, we have two gold now, yes, twenty-five more bricks soon, yes?"

Samantha answered, "Yes Krill. The two bricks you have now are yours to keep for your crew being delayed."

A slow smirk came to Krill's face, "Okay then...we wait."

Samantha pulled a portable ship-to-shore radio from the burlap bag.

"This radio is tuned to our frequency. Right now the pilot is held up in a motel just outside Lake Tahoe with one of our men. He will leave at 10:00 p.m. and the gold drop to us will take place at 11:50 p.m. sharp.

"We are only fifteen miles away. You will know the drop from the plane to our boat is under way when you see a flare fired from the Eureka Airport. As soon as we have recovered your gold, we will radio you that we are on the way for delivery. I know it's a lot of steps but please understand. Washington is going to be all over this one once it takes place and my employers must be able to express their condolences without looking over their shoulders to see who might be watching or asking questions. Now, are we clear on this?"

"Yes, we understand. We wait for gold," Krill answered.

Samantha responded, "Good. Glad we understand each other. Now are your shooters in place?"

Krill responded, "Shooters are good. We have people in place. Simple command by me and they operate undetected in your country. No trace to gold or your people."

Krill was reassuring his American counterparts that once the gold is delivered the plan goes into action almost immediately. He also wanted them to understand that once the payment is made there is no turning back on their plans.

Samantha stood to leave, "Good to know. In a few hours both our parts will be done. We can go about our business and let the next group take over."

The four Americans left the Russian boat for their own. Once the two boats were untied from each other, the Americans headed for the Eureka Harbor and then it was fifteen miles south to Sugarloaf Island. If all went as planned, they would be plucking a chest of gold from the angry West Coast ocean waters in just a few short hours.

CHAPTER 6

Cal Neva Casino
Friday 6:40 p.m. (PST) - 1962

Jake dialed the long distance number with deliberate motions.

"Hello" was the response on the other end of the receiver.

"Giovanni," Jake announced, "how's the pasta tonight?"

"Magnifico…baked to perfection. How's the kittens tonight?"

Jake responded, "We found the cat and he's back in the garage. All the kittens are safe except for one. He somehow got lost at the lake."

Giovanni asked, "Aw that's too bad. Which one?"

"The big one, the calico one, all the others are fine. They are purring so pretty. Hey listen Giovanni, I gotta run. I just called to let you know all is fine. We'll catch up later."

"Okay Jake. Glad you found the cat okay. That would be very upsetting to have him missing. Kiss your mother for me."

Jake hung up the phone from his East Coast counterpart, Giovanni.

They had to speak in code because the Feds were working the phone taps hard on the East Coast. They both knew the meals were the code names for the plan and the cat was Steve. The kittens stood for Jake's people and the lost calico was code for taking out Marty.

Next, Jake called Billy at the motel.

Billy answered the phone in anticipation of Jake's call, "Yeah."

"Listen Billy…make sure we have a good watch on the bird tonight. We can't screw this up. Do you understand?"

Billy smiled and asked, "Boss, who's the best you got? No worries, okay? I'll go over everything with our pilot friend. He will know the rules and know there are no second chances."

Billy made his hand into a gun and pointed it at Steve. While mimicking pulling the trigger, his mouth formed a very sinister smile.

"Billy, I can always count on you. Call me when the birds in the air."

"Will do," Billy answered.

He hung up the phone without saying a word. He just stared at Steve, curious as to what was on his mind.

Pacific Ocean - California Coast
Friday 7:05 p.m. (PST) - 1962

Out on the Russian trawler, Krill, Stanislav, and Mikhail were discussing the turn of events.

"Sure we have gold but why are they late with payoff?" Mikhail asked from the bunk he was half lying on.

"I don't like plan," he continued.

Krill answered, "We keep close watch on Americans. Yes, they make us nervous but we have big payoff coming."

Stanislav chimed in, "Without full payoff we cannot return to our country. I do not trust American woman. Maybe we leave now."

Krill slammed his fist hard on the table and threw his shot glass to the floor shattering it in several pieces. The glass shards slide across the galley floor and came to rest against the walls. At the same time, he was shouting at his fellow comrades.

"Enough! We wait for Americans to return. If we are double-crossed, they will never see their homeland again. Now quiet! We wait."

Mikhail and Stanislav quietly backed off their complaining.

Krill stared at the two gold bars glistening on the galley table. He was imagining what his life would be like once this hit was completed. Would he be able to live out his dreams or would he constantly be on the lookout? Would the American government track his involvement in this or could he quietly retire to a country villa somewhere in his country?

The shimmering gold loomed too large in Krill's mind to supersede reason. It was no longer about the President of the United States. It was no longer about the powerful people in his organization. It was no longer even about his crew. It was all about the gold that captured his very essence.

Pacific Ocean - Eureka Harbor, California
Friday 7:12 p.m. (PST) - 1962

Don Carlo guided the American boat toward the Eureka, CA harbor. Samantha would be dropped there and stationed at the airport to watch for Steve's arrival. This would be the final checkpoint before the gold drop.

Samantha poured herself a cup of coffee and sat at the galley table downstairs. The tension of all this was beginning to show on her face. She sipped her coffee, set it on the table, and rubbed her hands together trying to ease the tension.

She was a long way from her home in Minneapolis. Her husband thought she still worked for a national historical magazine. He accepted the fact that her occupation took her many places around the world. However, little did he know she had left the job a couple of years beforehand. She allowed him to believe she still worked there. It had become a front to cover her real reasons for traveling. He had no interest in history, so he and her job never collided.

Samantha was recruited by a known mob associate. Her womanly figure with long dark hair was exactly what the mob needed for effectively negotiating deals. Her beauty captured the hearts of many. It did not matter the job Samantha had to do, she always delivered.

She met the man one evening while on a business trip to Chicago. She was there gathering information for an article she was writing about the Great Chicago Fire of 1871. She had finished for the day and decided to stay at her hotel for the evening to relax. She was tired of running back and forth and was looking forward to a quiet dinner alone.

She was at her table in the hotel restaurant when the charming individual, who was seated at the table opposite of hers, smiled at her. She innocently returned the smile. Soon the man made small comments to her about the Chicago area. The conversation soon turned to him asking her why she was sitting alone having dinner in Chicago. She had a free and adventurous spirit. She could not resist telling him her discoveries about the Chicago Fire.

She was vulnerable that evening for whatever reason. Maybe it was the exhaustion she felt or maybe it was the disconnect she was feeling from her husband. Regardless, after dinner the man invited her to the hotel bar for a drink. Samantha had second thoughts but accepted anyway.

The two of them talked well into the morning. He noticed Samantha's flamboyant nature and her quest to be somebody. He felt confident enough to tell her about his business. It was not a typical job description. The man was heavily entrenched in the underworld. By the end of the conversation that evening she had become so intrigued with the man's stories and adventures that she gave into his offer of money, fame, and a life full of the unexpected.

The money was more than she could pass up. By the time she returned to Minneapolis, she had determined to quit her job but not say anything to her husband. He would not approve of her new lifestyle. Nevertheless, to keep the marriage somewhat alive, she would make him believe she was still working her historical writer's position.

Life was not the same after that. It was a world of travel, mystery, and being involved in things she never dreamed of. The money was great and over the next couple of years she became very good at what she did. Most people she met were easily convinced to see things her way.

Negotiations were her specialty. When the mob needed concessions from certain entities, Samantha was called on to negotiate with charm. Her charisma was infectious in obtaining the correct results.

One thing she did not count on was becoming pregnant a couple months earlier. It was after one of her long trips when she returned home. Her husband had dinner and roses waiting when she arrived. She was touched and for an evening, in her mind, she left her underworld lifestyle and returned to her husband and a home.

It lasted for an evening but soon she was off again. She hid the morning sickness but wondered when her stomach began to show how she was going to hide that from her employers.

Vinnie was on deck finishing the last of his cigarette and watching the waves meet the horizon. He had made sure all was ready with the landing skiff and headed for the galley for a cup of coffee. He was in high spirits that evening. He skipped every other step going down as he quickly jumped to the galley floor.

"Hey Samantha. I finished with the skiff and thought I would do the same…you know...get a cup of coffee. We do have a few hours to wait."

"Vinnie, are you sure you, Little Al, and Don Carlo are going to be able to locate that raft with the gold?" asked Samantha.

"Sure, no problem. We're going to be in place by the time that plane swings by. Not a chance we'll miss it. Why Samantha dear...do I detect worry in the Queen of Negotiations? What's up with that?"

"Sit down Vinnie," Samantha told him.

Vinnie finished pouring a cup of coffee and straddled the chair across from her.

"Vinnie," Samantha began, "this is a big responsibility we have going on here. I'm sure it's going to work but if something should happen to me, I don't want my husband to know the truth about my occupation. I need him to think I went to my grave doing historical work for the magazine. Will you make sure that happens?"

Vinnie knew Samantha's background. He knew the game she was playing at home.

"Of course Samantha, you know I would. We're in this together and we're going to pull it off without a hitch. Why the worry?"

"I'm pregnant," Samantha blurted.

Vinnie was in midstream of a sip of coffee when Samantha made the announcement. He slowly lowered the cup to the table. The shock on his face was clearly visible.

"Is it...you know...?"

She stopped him in mid-sentence.

"Yes, it's my husband's! I may do some crazy things but I don't mess around on him."

"Okay, just wanted to make sure," Vinnie backtracked.

"Sometimes I can't believe I entered this lifestyle," Samantha told him.

"I always thought I would have the perfect little marriage, the perfect little house, with the perfect little picket fence surrounding it. But I guess my desire for adventure washed that away. Somewhere along the way, I lost it.

"Vinnie, this is just for your ears only. Once we're done with this job and we're paid, I'm not sure I can continue. I'm going to have a kid for God's sake! I can't be toting guns around the country."

A lone tear trickled down her cheek as she continued.

"I don't want my child to know what I have done. I need to find a way out. That's not going to be easy, but I have to. I need to get back to my white picket fence and be normal. My child deserves it. My husband deserves it and I deserve it."

Vinnie sat stunned at what Samantha was telling him. He always looked up to her as a strong person and now that persona in his mind was changing.

"Samantha...one day at a time, okay...one day at a time. This job pays well enough that you won't have to worry about your tomorrows. But if you get out, can you live knowing our employers may be waiting around the next corner? Once you're in, you are really in! Breaking away isn't going to be easy."

Samantha did not need to be told the consequences of breaking free. She had seen the pain that can be inflicted on individuals wanting to make a break for it.

With compassion in her voice, she told Vinnie, "I know. But I've got to figure it out. Tell you what, I won't make any decisions tonight. We'll get this job done and go from there. I won't even tell you if I make a break from it. I don't want to put you in that position of knowing anything. If you're ever questioned you can easily say, *I had no idea.*"

Vinnie just smiled and said, "Nice weather tonight for a boat ride. Wouldn't you say?"

He wanted off the subject. Both smiled as Samantha wiped the tear from her cheek.

Samantha gathered her emotions and went upstairs on deck. Don Carlo was just entering the Eureka Harbor and would soon dock to allow Samantha to go ashore. Boat traffic in the harbor was light that evening. That was okay with the crew. They did not need any eyes watching their moves tonight.

Samantha was going to be the final checkpoint at the Eureka Municipal Airport. She would wait for Steve to fly over and then radio the boys on the boat that the gold was on its way.

Don Carlo masterfully guided the boat into the first open dock he came to. Samantha gathered a portable radio and a trigger mechanism and headed for the gangplank. She paused and turned to her crew. She smiled and was about to say something but decided to just turn and walk away.

Samantha walked to a car that was left there for her. She pulled the keys from the sun visor, started the car, and drove to the airport. She wondered if she should have said what was on her mind. Samantha decided her decision to wait until after the gold was dropped was an okay choice.

With Vinnie and Little Al onboard the American boat, Don Carlo backed away from the dock and headed for Sugarloaf Island, 15 miles to the south. The long night was just beginning.

Washington, DC
Friday 7:16 p.m. (PST) - 1962

The lobby at Vinchelli's Restaurant, located on Pennsylvania Avenue a few miles from the White House, was more crowded than normal for a Friday night. Wait time for a table was easily surpassing an hour. High style men and women milled around, drinks in hand, laughing and talking the evening away while waiting for their table.

The Senator entered the lobby with a concerned look on his face. The lobby receptionist recognized him and quickly picked up the phone and called the back office.

"Just wanted to let you know he's here in the lobby," the clerk said.

Lou hurriedly left his office for the lobby. He saw the Senator headed in his direction.

"Senator, it's so nice to see you this evening."

The two men greeted each other with a handshake.

"Right this way, we have a table waiting for you."

Lou led the Senator through the lobby past the other patrons to a booth a good distance from the main traffic. It had a curtain that could be closed for semi-private meetings.

The Senator sat down and Lou sat across from him. Lou motioned the waiter to bring a bottle of wine. There was no mention of what type. The waiter knew when Lou snapped his fingers it meant to bring only the best in the house.

Lou had an uneasy feeling about this meeting. Usually the Senator was full of small talk but this time he seemed preoccupied. Lou was troubled by the way the Senator was acting.

The waiter returned, uncorked the wine, and poured the Senator and Lou a glass. He set the bottle on the table. Lou motioned the waiter to wait for a moment. He turned to the Senator.

"We have terrific lobster ravioli tonight. The cream sauce is an old family recipe. Would you like to try it?"

The Senator said, "Yes, but make mine a half order. I don't have much of an appetite tonight."

The waiter acknowledged the order and walked away. Lou stood and closed the curtain. The Senator's tone in his voice indicated this called for a private meeting.

"So what's up Harry?" Lou asked the Senator.

The Senator spoke in a low tone.

"It's not pretty Lou. It's just not pretty. The Senate Ethics Committee is meeting tonight in a closed session. It seems someone has gotten a hold of a private report on the Ohio Union Pension Fund. They are questioning campaign contributions."

"Campaign contributions? What in the world for?" Lou asked.

"Well Lou, they've already examined the public documents but these private documents they got their hands on aren't adding up. These private trips and parties you guys afforded certain high profile people of whom I will not name were not recorded on the public documents, but references were made in the private documents. Do you know what that does to our arrangement?"

Lou just sighed in disgust as the Senator continued.

"There isn't a one of those guys that will admit they were not on the receiving end of those gifts. They have no reason to deny it! Furthermore, when they start naming names, some of these junior politicians are going to start voting for cutbacks in certain…shall we say...preferential government bonuses. Some may even roll over and call for an immediate investigation of the upper management of these pensions."

"Harry, how did this happen? Who called the Ethics Committee to session?"

The Senator looked Lou right in the eye and sternly said, "The top Lou...the very top!"

"Ah Harry, this is bad. This is really bad."

"I know," the Senator responded.

Lou continued, "Those travel documents your counterpart got me...we're still good on those, aren't we?"

"As far as I know Lou. As-far-as-I-know!"

The men continued the evening mostly in silence. There was nothing more to be said. Lou knew what plans were in motion out on the West Coast but was not about to admit at this point to any knowledge of those plans.

Pacific Ocean - Sugarloaf Island
Friday 7:45 p.m. (PST) - 1962

With the cover of darkness, Don Carlo pulled the boat within 100 yards of the northwest side of Sugarloaf Island. There he dropped anchor hoping to hold the ship in place against the wind and currents.

The anchor sank into forty feet of ocean water and lodged in the sandy bed below. Don Carlo retracted the anchor chain pulling the anchor tight against the ocean floor.

He cut the main engines allowing the sound of the crashing waves to penetrate the night air. He sat in the darkness wondering whether this was all going to work or if it would be a total catastrophe. He wondered if it did work, what would be the consequences and if it didn't, would he spend his life on the run?

Vinnie prepared the skiff that would be used to recover the gold once it was dropped by Steve. If all went well, Little Al, Don Carlo, and he would motor around the corner of the island and tow the crate of gold that would be floating on the raft back to the American boat. Steve and the plane would be shattered into pieces by the bomb exploding and would be scattered on the ocean floor below.

The three would use the ships onboard winch to pluck the crate of gold from the sea and set it on the boat deck. Their job would be almost complete at that point. From there it would be a quick fifteen miles and a swift delivery to the Russian ship.

Grass Valley, California
Friday 7:56 p.m. (PST) - 1962

Luke arrived at the Nevada County Air Park. He parked at the end of Runway 25. It was a desolate area and would be a good view of Steve buzzing the airfield.

He kept the two-way radio off for the time being. He knew Steve was not due to fly over until 10:35 p.m. He did not want to hear any chatter that may be taking place over the radio.

Luke stared at the electronic trigger switch Billy had given him at the motel. He wondered if he would be able to push the button, triggering the plane to explode if Steve did not follow directions. He really was just a gopher for the organization and actually never killed a man before.

Luke knew that if he followed through with this it could get him closer to Jake. He wanted to become like his peers but he was questioning whether he could actually go through with the deed.

As the AM radio softly played its tunes, Luke nestled in and watched the stars. He had a lot on his mind. Protecting his interests was one of them. In a couple hours, things were going to get pretty harried.

CHAPTER 7

The Motel Room
Friday 8:16 p.m. (PST) - 1962

Steve was still sitting in the chair when he heard the car door slam. He was intently watching the clock on the nightstand wondering when something was going to happen. The suspense of waiting for when things would start was pushing his emotions to the limit.

A heavy knock on the door once again brought Billy into action. He approached the motel door.

"Yeah, Tony, is that you?"

"Yep, sure is Billy. It's time. Let's get a move on it."

Billy gathered the duffle bag from the corner and told Steve to get up. *This must be it,* Steve thought. Things appeared to be happening. Both men headed for the door.

Steve's heart was beginning to pound. He had so much uncertainty about what was coming. There was no question in his mind that these men were serious. This was not a game. He still had no clue how or when he might end this or even if he could.

Billy opened the door and pushed Steve to the back seat of the Lincoln parked in front of the motel room. Tony was already in the driver's seat acting restless and impatient.

No one spoke as they headed for the Lake Tahoe Airport. The tires of the big car made a slapping sound on the pavement as the wheels crossed the tar cracks in the road.

Billy puffed continually on his cigarettes during the entire ride. Steve had not seen Billy portray anything other than a non-caring, rough individual. Although Billy tried to remain calm, Steve could now see the man was tense and nervous.

The airport was dark when the Lincoln rounded the corner into the parking lot. Tony drove the car to a flimsy gate on the south edge of the airport. He pulled up to the gate, placed the car in park, got out, and lifted the wooden arm that blocked the entrance.

Steve's heart pounded even harder. The headlights slowly started to illuminate the dark object parked in the back corner of the airport.

Soon Steve had full view of the *Helldiver* aircraft he had flown earlier in the day. The plane looked menacing sitting there darkened by the night sky, illuminated only by the car headlights.

The Lincoln carrying the men stopped directly in front of the plane. Tony cut the ignition and turned the headlights off. The silence was deafening. The only sound that could be heard was Billy puffing on his cigarette.

Billy and Tony looked in all directions before deciding to exit the vehicle. They wanted to make sure their tracks were covered.

"What do you think Billy? I don't see anyone, do you?" Tony asked.

"We will just sit tight for a minute. I want to make sure we are alone. I don't want anyone snooping around our business," Billy answered.

Billy smoked another cigarette as the men waited. Once finished he simply said, "Okay, let's go."

Steve tried to exit the car but Billy told him to sit tight. He instructed Steve that when it is time for him to get out, he would let him know.

Billy and Tony exited the car. Tony opened the trunk and both men grabbed flashlights. Tony also grabbed a hammer and a small ladder. He placed the ladder to the side of the plane, climbed to the top, and slid the canopy open.

Steve watched as Tony climbed inside the cockpit with the hammer. He positioned himself and took a mighty swing at the dash. The smack of the hammer left no question in Steve's mind that the man's intent was to destroy something.

Steve thought to himself, *what the heck is he doing?*

Billy pulled the duffle bag from the car. He fumbled inside and retrieved what looked like a portable radio. He handed it to Tony who placed it in the cockpit.

Tony climbed down, threw the hammer in the trunk and joined Billy at the plane. They both talked out of the range of Steve's hearing.

"Okay Tony, let's double check everything. First, the bomb has been loaded and you're sure it's set to go off at 11:52 p.m. tonight, right?"

"Right," Tony responded.

"And the receiver is set to the frequency of the triggers if we need to blow it sooner, correct?"

"Right again."

"The crate is secured to the bomb deployment armature?"

"Yep."

"Finally, the chute and the raft are rigged to deploy upon the release of the crate, correct?"

"Billy, I know you're just covering your tracks on this but everything is a go on our side, okay? I have double-checked and rechecked all of this, including all the radios being tuned to the correct frequency. That swing with the hammer took out the planes radio. There is no way for him to contact anyone but us."

"Okay Tony. I guess it's time to brief this yo-yo on what he is to do."

Billy picked up his flashlight and rummaged through his duffle bag. He pulled out a map for Steve to follow. He placed the map on the car's front hood and motioned Steve to join him at the front of the car.

Steve took a deep breath and exited the car as requested by Billy. He began briefing Steve on what he was to do.

"Okay, here is the plan. As you know you are going to drop this gold off the shoreline of Sugarloaf Island."

Billy illuminated the map with the flashlight and pointed out Sugarloaf Island. Steve was fighting to concentrate on what he was being told. The explosives he knew were onboard shadowed his attention span. Billy continued with the instructions.

"Now you are carrying a lot of gold worth a lot of money and we are not going to just turn you loose to fly off to who knows where. We have our own precautions in place. So here is what you are going to do.

"When you leave here, fly 290° for 61 miles to the Nevada County Airport. Make a low-level pass over the runway. You can't miss it. It's the only runway at the airport.

"Next, fly 321° for 62 miles to the Chico Municipal Airport. Again, make a low-level pass over the runway. Then fly 343° for 64 miles to the Redding Municipal Airport. Like before, make a low-level pass."

Steve interrupted, "Maybe you can tell me the purpose of flying down these runways at such a low-level?"

Billy sarcastically answered, "Because I told you to. Don't fight me on this. We have plans for you if you do not follow instructions.

"Finally, I want you to fly 378° for 98 miles to the Eureka Airport. When you arrive in Eureka, make a low-level pass and at the end of the runway climb to 2,000 feet. Circle the airport and wait for a signal flare to be fired. Then turn south, and descend to 300 feet. Follow the coast until you arrive at Sugarloaf Island. You must arrive precisely at 11:50 p.m. Make your drop at the base on the east side and then...uh return to Eureka and land. Now you do know how to use the bomb bay doors and drop this thing, right?"

Steve looked at Billy and wondered how this man could be so cold-hearted. He knew he was sending Steve to a violent death. How could he be so greedy as to not care about life?

Steve was determined more than ever to survive this dilemma. Not only survive, but also make sure the people involved paid dearly for their greed. He had no love loss for the people who were pushing him around.

Billy folded the map neatly. He handed the folded map and a flashlight to Steve.

Steve sarcastically asked, "That's it...a map and a flashlight? You expect me to pinpoint four locations in the dark with nothing more than a heading and a given distance? Have you ever flown a plane? Don't you understand that what you are asking me to do leaves a lot of room for mistakes?"

Billy folded his arms and rubbed his chin with his left hand. Finally, he answered with a bit of an attitude.

"Yeah, that's it. This is all you get. Oh, but wait, we have a couple of other things for you. The radio in the plane…smashed. You get a hand-held portable tuned to our frequency and only our frequency. We didn't want to take the chance of you relaying our plans to whoever would listen.

"Secondly, should you just bolt or not make your destination on time…we have a little send off for you and it goes off with a blast so large there won't be enough left to fill a sandwich bag.

"Now do you want to complain further about having to dead-reckon this bad boy or are you going to call on that expertise of yours that everyone has raved about?"

Steve became extremely agitated and was about to lose his temper when a large Cadillac drove up and stopped next to the Lincoln.

The rear door opened and Jake stepped out. Steve wondered why he was showing up. The big man walked up to Steve and put his hand on his shoulder as if he were an old friend.

"Hey listen," he said to Steve.

"We kind of got off to a bad start. You can imagine my frustration when you didn't show on time?"

Steve said nothing.

Jake continued, "Anyway, don't let it bother you. We're good. You pull this off as planned and maybe we can find you a place in our organization. We're always looking for new good men."

Steve responded sarcastically, "Yeah, I bet you are."

Jake laughed and slapped him on the back and simply said, "We'll talk."

He turned to Billy, paused, and gave a serious look. Jake left without saying another word.

Chico, California
Friday 9:43 p.m. (PST) - 1962

Frankie dropped Lester off in the parking lot of the Chico Municipal Airport. Earlier that day a car had been stationed in the parking lot for Lester to use.

Lester drove the car out to Runway 31L and there he waited. He waited for Steve to make the low-level pass over the runway signifying all was on track.

Frankie continued on to the Redding Municipal Airport to do his watch. By the time he arrived at Runway 34, Steve had already left the Lake Tahoe Airport and was in the air on his way to a very eventful evening.

Lake Tahoe Airport, California
Friday 9:51 p.m. (PST) - 1962

Steve gathered the map and flashlight and headed for the ladder leading to the cockpit. As he put his step on the first rung, Billy called out to Steve.

"Hey, one more thing, you don't want to try the bomb doors until you actually have to use them. You only have one opportunity."

Steve thought to himself, *no kidding Sherlock.*

He knew Billy had no idea that Steve had knowledge about the bomb going off two minutes after he dropped the gold. He had no idea Steve knew about the attempt on JFK's life.

Steve climbed to the cockpit and placed his things inside. He returned to the ground to complete the usual preflight aircraft checklist. Although this was nothing like a conventional flight, flying was flying and shortcuts were not part of flying.

Steve returned to the cockpit. He lit the flying cocoon with his flashlight.

He saw the smashed radio. The plane looked as though it did when he first picked it up from George Masters. Everything was the same except for one thing. The carving on the dash, *ST MPLS 62,* was missing. It stood out like a sore thumb when Steve flew the plane earlier. He wondered how it could have disappeared. Although he wondered, deep down he expected it to reappear at some point.

Steve's adrenaline was starting to rise. What a tough job lay ahead of him. The *Curtiss Helldiver* was a dive-bomber and would be able to pinpoint the drop okay, but normally this was done with a two-man crew; a pilot and a radio operator/gunner. He would have to go it alone. In addition, he was only about two hours away from death by a bomb blast…two hours to figure out how he would save himself and possibly the President.

Steve pulled the seatbelt tight and readied himself for flight. He switched on the magnetos, primed the fuel system, and hit the starter. Within seconds the 2,000 horsepower Pratt & Whitney engine sprang to life. The sound pierced the night air as the engine started its warm up phase.

Once again, the plane inched forward with Steve as the pilot. The plane crept toward the runway on its way to an uncertain destiny. It was an uncertain destiny for what Steve thought the future held as well.

During the aircraft run-up prior to take-off, Steve methodically scanned the instrument panel. He knew there was no chance of dropping out of sight. The plane was wired to blow if it did not make the checkpoints. He had to find a way to bring the aircraft down in sight of his tormentors and make a last ditch effort to stop this madness.

Steve made a final tug on his seatbelts and headed for the departure end of the runway. Time had come to begin this journey. He pushed the throttle to the firewall and once again the aircraft responded to Steve's command.

The take-off roll was smooth and straight. The old warbird effortlessly lifted itself to flight. It was now or never for Steve.

The plane rose quickly as Steve pulled back on the yoke. He headed in a northwesterly direction. Once he was at an altitude sufficient to clear the mountains, he leveled off.

It was important to keep as close to the ground as possible. The dead-reckoning he had to do was a little bit more difficult because the growth and ground lighting was less than what he was accustomed to seeing.

A short time after leveling off he began a slow decent to his first checkpoint, the Nevada County Air Park. It was like finding a needle in a haystack.

After Billy had visibly confirmed Steve's take-off, he radioed the others that the operation was underway. The two then left the airport with Tony driving. The plan was that the two would head for the Eureka Airport to meet up with the rest of the crew. They were going to celebrate in style once the operation was completed.

Eureka Airport, California
Friday 10:01 p.m. (PST) - 1962

Samantha parked near the edge of the runway at the Eureka Municipal Airport and waited for her part to take place in the plan. She had never met Steve and had no clue as to his flying abilities. All she knew was he was a pilot that could drop a bomb precisely where needed.

Her thoughts turned to what his physical appearance might be. *Was he tall? Short? Thin? Does he have hair?* Her thought pattern was scattered that evening. She had a lot on her mind.

Samantha turned her radio to the frequency of the American boat.

"Don Carlo, come in, over," she radioed.

"Don Carlo here, over."

"I know we were concerned earlier that the surf would be rough. Is all okay, over?" Samantha asked.

"A-Okay here. Surf is light and we have no drift, over."

"10-4. I'll be in touch as soon as I see the bird headed your way, over."

"10-4, over." Don Carlo responded.

Samantha laid the radio handset down and watched the surf at the end of the runway crash to the shore. She thought of her crew and her departure from the boat earlier. She thought that maybe she should have said what was on her mind when she walked from the boat to the shore. She dismissed her thoughts knowing she would soon see them again after the gold drop.

Grass Valley, California
Friday 10:10 p.m. (PST) - 1962

It did not take Steve long to cover the approximate 60 miles to the Nevada County Air Park. Finding the airport in darkness proved to be another matter. Steve turned the plane toward the northwest and searched for the runway. He circled several times before spotting his mark.

Banking the plane to the left and dropping the altitude to a low-level pass, he zoomed down the runway 100 feet above the ground.

Getting to the end, he pulled back on the stick and sent the plane upward once more.

Luke keyed the mic on his two-way radio.

"Nevada Air Park calling Central, over."

Billy pulled his radio closer while Tony drove toward the Eureka Airport.

"Central here, go ahead Nevada Air Park, over."

"The bird has made contact. All okay, over."

"10-4 Nevada Air Park. You know where to meet, over."

"10-4, out."

Luke started his car and headed for the rendezvous point.

Steve was listening to the conversation intently on the portable radio he was given by Billy and Tony. He wondered whether he had passed his first test or if a sudden and deadly explosion would end his life. Steve kept flying without incident but not without a huge amount of stress.

Steve thought about what Billy had said over the two-way radio regarding a meeting place somewhere. That was going to be some useful information if he could find out where.

Steve turned his attention back to flying. His next stop was the Chico Municipal Airport, approximately 60 miles to the northwest. Time was of the essence. He had to make Eureka by 11:30 p.m.

CHAPTER 8

Washington, DC
Friday 10:02 p.m. (PST) - 1962

The Senator pulled his car into the drive of the abandoned steel mill on the Lower West Side. It was dark and the mill had been left unattended for many years. He turned his headlights off and traveled the final 200 yards in darkness.

A dark colored green sedan drove up to meet the Senator's car in the same fashion as the Senator. It was several minutes before the occupants of either car stepped out of their vehicles. The cloak of darkness was essential. There could be no one in the area to see this meeting take place.

Two ominous men in long trench coats and fedoras greeted the Senator as he stepped from his car.

"So Senator, do you think he bought it?"

The two FBI agents were eager to hear his answer. Several months earlier the FBI had received a tip that the mob was very dissatisfied in their inability to control some of the politicians on Capitol Hill. The agency took this threat very seriously. It became a national security threat when it was revealed the President was the intended target.

The mob wanted to protect their interests they had worked so hard to attain. By making a hit on the President, they were convinced that everything would settle down to normal. With the elimination of JFK, they thought the political masses would be silenced.

At that time, with the help of the CIA, the FBI concocted *Operation Smoke Out.* The first phase of the operation was to plant falsified information into the mob, hoping to rat out the players. They needed to find out who was calling the shots on this one.

They knew Lou, the manager at Vinchelli's Restaurant, was a made-man. It was a hunch they could get something started with him by gaining his confidence and spreading rumors that certain politicians were going to roll over on the bribe money they had accepted for their information and silence.

Lou's restaurant was popular with the good guys and with *people of interest.* It was here the FBI decided to begin *Operation Smoke Out.*

Lou seemed to be the most likely to have loose lips. With him being somewhat of a drama queen, they knew the rumors would be spread to the correct parties.

The FBI was anxious to act quickly on the tips they had received months earlier. The Senator was enlisted to get close to Lou over a period of time and infiltrate the organization by feeding false information.

The Senator looked around making sure no one could be seen.

"Yeah, I think Lou really bought it," the Senator said.

"In fact I think he bought it a long time ago. I just have a feeling something is going down. I'm nervous guys. This isn't my line of work! Lou got very quiet after he asked about the President's itinerary. Yeah…I think it's going down."

The Senator was nervous and jumpy. He was regretting his decision to help the FBI in this sting operation.

"Calm down Senator! Look around. Do you see anyone? Harry, we've taken great strides to keep your identity covered. Don't walk on us now."

The Senator looked down and kicked a rock that was at his feet.

"I know guys. It's just…it's just I'm scared, okay! These guys aren't playground bullies. They are for real. They take torture and murder to the extreme. And-I-am-lying to them!" the Senator said emphatically.

The other FBI agent spoke up.

"Listen, intelligence is telling us we are close to cracking this case. You think, and we also think, this is about to go down and you're right, we are so close. One more meeting with Lou and I think he will spill his guts on everything. You have masterfully gained his confidence. We have made sure everything you told him could be verified with others who are not involved in this operation."

The other FBI agent chimed in.

"Here's what we need to have happen. We want you to go back to Vinchelli's tonight. You are going to act as if you've had one too many to drink. Before arriving, spill some booze on your clothes, loosen the tie, un-tuck your shirt, then go find Lou. Tell him you can't sleep and you need to know when their plans are going down so you can make sure to have an alibi. Just act drunk. You got that?"

The Senator took a deep breath and sighed.

"Okay guys. One more time but this is it. I'm out after this. I'm going to take a long vacation and get away from it all. This is too much pressure on me. Do you understand? Too much pressure!"

"Don't worry Senator. We've got your back."

The men parted ways and returned to their vehicles. The Senator waited for the FBI agents to leave first. After a few moments, he too left. While exiting the abandoned mill he passed an older man pushing a shopping cart filled with musty relics. They glanced at one another and the Senator drove off headed for Vinchelli's while the old man quickened his pace.

Washington, DC
Friday 10:15 p.m. (PST) - 1962

The old man pushed his shopping cart at a fast clip to the corner and down a narrow street to a local pub. He briskly walked inside to a pay phone tucked back in the corner next to a stack of beer cases. He fumbled in his pocket looking for a dime to use in the pay phone. He pulled the dime and a crumbled piece of paper from his pocket. He deposited the money and methodically dialed the number printed on the wrinkled scrap of paper.

After a few rings, the other phone was answered.

"Vinchelli's, may I help you?"

The old man's voice crackled as he spoke.

"Mr. Lou please."

"Who's calling?"

"Willy."

"Willy who?"

"Just tell Mr. Lou, Willy. He'll know me."

The person on the other end went to track down Lou in the restaurant.

Lou had come to know Willy from a local network of snitches that worked for the mob. Lou would give food to him in exchange for Willy keeping his eyes and ears open out on the street.

Lou picked up the phone.

"Willy, why are you calling me?"

"Mr. Lou…he's dirty! I just saw him talking with the suits."

"Dirty? Who's dirty Willy?"

"That Senator guy that's been hanging out at your place. Big meeting just took place with the Feds at the old abandoned mill on 6th Street."

"Are you sure Willy? I've got to know for sure that you're right."

"Yep, sure as the day is blue. I crept up on them whiles they was talking. Something about the Senator is scared and that he's been lying to ya."

"Willy, are you positive?"

"Sure am."

"Thanks and stop by tomorrow. I'll have a great meal waiting for you."

"Okay, Mr. Lou."

Willy hung up the phone and returned to his shopping cart not realizing the damage he had just done. He continued down the street picking through the discards of other people.

Lou hung the phone up and quickly went to his office. He poured himself a drink and wondered what his next move would be. Somehow he had to get word to the West Coast that the organization had been infiltrated. The Senator's actions could have disastrous consequences.

Vinchelli's Restaurant - Washington, DC
Friday 10:20 p.m. (PST) - 1962

The Senator did what the FBI agents had asked of him. He did his best to stumble into the lobby of Vinchelli's in a drunken stupor. He wanted to look, act, and smell the part. In his car, he had opened a bottle of wine he had received from one of his constituents and smeared it on his jacket to authenticate his performance.

"Where's my friend Lou? Lou…hey Lou, it's me," the Senator announced in the lobby with a slurred voice.

Lou quickly came to the lobby and led the Senator as quietly as possible to his office. He passed two large men standing at the bar. Lou snapped his fingers for them to follow. The Senator had no idea Lou was on to him.

Lou entered his office. The two large men followed and closed the door behind them. At that moment, Lou turned violent and shoved the Senator to the chair. He grabbed his shirt and ripped it open thinking he may be wearing a wire.

The Senator was startled. He yelled, "Lou...Lou what is this?"

"What is this? What is this you ask?" Lou screamed.

He swung his fist to the right and caught the Senator directly in the jaw cracking it in two places. The Senator was stunned and could not speak because of the pain. He looked at Lou with fear in his eyes. The Senator no longer was acting drunk. His worst fears had come true.

Lou continued, "You dare come in here and lie to me!"

The Senator tried to speak, "Lou…"

Before anymore could be said, Lou's rage took over. He pummeled the Senator with a few more blows. He then got up close to the Senator's face and looked at his fearful eyes. He spoke in a slow and evil tone.

"Yes Senator. Look at me in fear!"

He grabbed the Senator's collar and pulled him even closer.

"I trusted you and you lie to me? You sell me down the river? You're in bed with the Feds? How dare you! Yes, Senator you look at these eyes. These are the eyes that you will remember for eternity. The last eyes you will ever see!"

Lou took one final swing knocking the Senator to the floor and rendering him unconscious. He turned to the two thugs standing to the side and barked his orders.

"Take him to the 5th Street Bridge. Wait until you see the bus coming from the other side, then throw him over and let him *catch the bus* face first. Now take the lousy creep out the back door and get him out of here for good!"

The two thugs did as they were told. Lou poured himself another drink and tried to figure out how he was going to stop this ambush.

The headlines the next morning would read *Senator Commits Suicide...Jumps in front of a bus while in a drunken stupor.*

Chico, California
Friday 10:22 p.m. (PST) - 1962

Steve flew toward the Chico Municipal Airport. He watched the California valley floor go by. He did his best to recognize the landmarks and correlate them with the map he had. Soon he would be passing his second checkpoint and he still did not have a plan in place.

Up ahead the Chico Airport came into view. He could see a car sitting at the end of the runway facing away from the direction Steve was coming from. He figured this must be Lester at his checkpoint.

Time to have a little fun with this bozo, Steve thought.

Steve was a masterful pilot. He dropped the aircraft down to the lowest possible altitude. He pushed the throttles to the firewall and brought the speed to 275 miles per hour.

Because the plane was going so fast and close to the ground, Lester did not hear Steve approaching from behind. The sound wave was a short distance behind the fast moving plane.

Lester was about to take a sip of coffee when the plane reached the rear of the car. In a gigantic whoosh, Steve flew the plane 25 feet directly over Lester's car at 275 miles per hour. The concussion and sound wave rocked the car so hard Lester spilled the hot coffee all over himself.

He shook his fist and cursed at the plane. Steve blasted the plane skyward and on to his next checkpoint. He could not see the surprise on Lester's face but he knew it was there. With a smirk on his face, he headed for Redding Municipal Airport.

Lester angrily snapped the radio-mic to his mouth. He was fuming with Steve for buzzing him and making him spill his coffee.

"Chico Municipal to central, over."

"Go ahead Chico, over."

"Our so called prized pilot just flew by. Buzzed my car too! He made me spill my coffee all over the front of me. I'm going to have to get a new shirt before heading for Trinidad, over."

Billy boiled with anger. After the gold drop, the plan was for everyone to meet in Eureka and then head north up the coast to Trinidad and chill for a bit until the heat blew over. That was not information to be openly exchanged over the radio.

"Chico…drop the conversation NOW, over and out!"

Lester did not answer. He knew he had screwed up by announcing the meeting point.

To Steve, it was just the information he needed. He knew he would arrive in Eureka before anyone else. If he was going to stop this madness, he thought he could catch a break there. He did not know Samantha was waiting for him.

Steve flew on to the next checkpoint, Redding Municipal Airport. He made the requested low-level pass, turned westward, and headed for the coast. Eureka was a short distance and Steve's mind was busy formulating a plan.

He came up with an idea that he thought just might work. As he flew over the Eureka Airport, he could flip the magneto switch back and forth causing the plane's engine to miss and backfire. If need be, he would radio the plane was having engine problems and that he was going to have to shut it down in Eureka. Should anyone be waiting on the ground they would certainly hear the engine misfiring and might lend leniency to pressing the destruct button for the plane.

This plan was not fool proof though. Steve had two concerns. First, if he flipped the magneto to make the engine backfire would he lose power completely? If he did, he would be too close to the ground to recover and a crash would be eminent.

Second, regardless what the plane did, would some idiot on the ground blow the plane? Would they even give him time to explain the planes malfunction?

Washington, DC
Friday 10:29 p.m. (PST) - 1962

Lou's hands shook as he dialed Giovanni's phone number. This whole plan had to stop before it was too late for the players involved.

Giovanni answered the phone, "Hello."

"Giovanni, its Lou. We've got some major problems here. Harry was dirty!"

"Lou...are you calling from the private line?"

"Of course," Lou replied.

Giovanni continued, "Then what do you mean, *Harry's dirty*?"

The tone of Lou's voice was becoming more excited as he continued with the conversation.

"Just what I said, the Senator is dirty. He's been working with the Feds all along. We need to shut this entire operation down. We can't afford to have this happen to us. We're gonna get---"

Giovanni interrupted, "Working with the Feds? That seems like some wrong information. How do you know this?"

"I've got a set of eyes on the street and he saw it go down."

"Is he reliable?" Giovanni asked.

"Been working for me for three years and hasn't failed me yet. We gotta shut this thing down. We're gonna have people crawling all over us on this."

"Lou...calm down. Let's not jump the gun just yet. Have you told the Senator anything about our operation on the West Coast?"

"No Giovanni, of course not. He knows we have plans but not the specifics. I just worked him for information."

Giovanni continued, "So you never said anything to the Senator specifically regarding our plans, right?"

"Right, not a word."

"Well has the uh...oh what shall I call it...the *situation* been silenced?"

"Yes, Giovanni. My guys have it all taken care of."

Giovanni thought about the ramifications of the Senator. If they stop now the Feds certainly would continue to infiltrate in some other way through some other person. If they continue as planned, the root of the problem would be taken care of. Giovanni decided it was best to continue with the plans as they were happening.

"Listen Lou, as long as nothing was said, they can't trace anything to us. Besides, it's too late now anyway. Plans are under way as we speak."

"You are going to have to cover your tracks on this one. You allowed this to happen. You fix it! If questioned, tell the Feds the Senator showed up making a scene, you sent him out the back door to get a cab to minimize the brunt of embarrassment, and that was the last you have seen of him. Also, keep your mouth shut on this. We do not need the rest of the guys being spooked. We have to play this cool. You got that?"

"Yes sir." Lou answered.

After they hung up the phone, Lou thought of the many conversations he had with the Senator. He knew he did not say anything incriminating to him. In addition, the Senator knew nothing about what was going down at that moment on the West Coast. However, the Senator did know something was going to happen and wondered if he had relayed that information to the Feds.

Lou poured himself another drink to calm down. His mind kept racing.

Were the Feds on the way? Was Giovanni now going to waste him? Who were his allies? Who were his enemies?

These were all questions that repeatedly ransacked his mind. His ability to think clearly was clouded with unanswered questions. He could not take the uncertainty in his life. He saw no way out.

He drank another shot of whiskey and opened the bottom drawer of his desk. From under a notebook he pulled the chrome-plated 38 revolver. He spun the barrel and laid it on his desk.

He did not want to…but he also could not face the thought of prison. He could not face the thought of a mob henchman possibly knocking on his doorstep. He had seen firsthand the ruthlessness these people possessed.

He felt trapped with no way out. Life of what he thought it to be had become an empty shell. In his mind, his choices in life had erased the ability to escape the consequences of those very choices.

He stood up from his desk and walked across the room to the shower he had installed in his office a few months earlier. Lou opened the door and turned the water on.

He then returned to his desk and picked up the revolver. It felt heavy in his hand. He walked the last ten steps of his life, opened the shower door, and stepped in.

Lou crumbled to the floor of the shower stall. The water quickly soaked his clothes. He heard nothing. He felt nothing. The water continued to run down his clothes and swirl with his blood on the shower floor before disappearing down the drain.

CHAPTER 9

Somewhere on the road in Northern California
Friday 10:31 p.m. (PST) - 1962

The headlights of the cars lit the tree line along the roadside. Billy had just answered Frankie's radio call from the Redding Municipal Airport that Steve had cleared the area and that he was on his way to Eureka.

Tony and Billy had not yet reached Redding and they were a good two hours from Eureka. Traffic was beginning to get scarce the further they drove toward the coast. Both men were tired. There had been a lot of planning and secrecy surrounding this hit.

Tony spoke first.

"Billy, do you think we'll be okay? I mean, this is the President. The Russians…the gold, this is big! There are so many people involved.

Are we going to have people breathing down our necks the rest of our lives?"

"Tony…I don't know. We are so far into it now we can't see daylight."

Billy sighed and continued the conversation.

"But we're going to be okay. The Russians, I'm sure, will take some heat but they will just run over the justice system claiming some international law to keep them out of the hot seat. No one is going to tie this back to us."

Tony answered, "I suppose you're right but gosh, people gotta keep their mouths shut. All it takes is one loose cannon to bring us all down."

Billy explained his take on it all.

"Jake has done his homework. He didn't get to be head of the West Coast by being a nice guy. He has covered his tracks well, you'll see. Plans have been made for loose cannons."

The two men drove on into the night. By now traffic on the road going to Eureka was nearly nonexistent.

The road made a bend and followed a riverbed. At a wide spot next to the river, Billy told Tony to pull the car over so he could stretch his legs. The riverbed was a good 25 feet below the shoulder of the road.

Tony stopped the car and Billy got out. He made sure his overcoat was not in the way of his gun holster. Tony waited in the car for Billy to relieve himself.

"Hey Tony," Billy called out.

"Why don't you jump in the passenger seat and I'll drive for awhile?"

Tony was tired and welcomed the opportunity. He exited the car and walked around the front. Billy walked from the rear around to the driver's door. Tony was about to open the passenger door when Billy called out again.

"Tony," he said in a sinister tone.

Tony looked up to see Billy with his pistol pointed directly at him. Looking down the barrel of a gun startled Tony.

"Hey, come on Billy, don't screw around like that. What's the matter with you? I don't want to play these games."

All was silent except for the cocking of the revolver with Billy's thumb.

"You were right Tony."

"What's that?" Tony answered.

The single gunshot echoed through the woods. A flock of birds scattered from their resting place. An owl began to hoot loudly in the distance.

"You were so right Tony...too many players involved..."

The lifeless body of Tony tumbled down the embankment into the river. It became entangled in a downed tree lying beneath the water.

Billy climbed in the car and drove off. He left the body of Tony behind in the darkness and hidden from sight. His thoughts turned inward.

With Marty and Tony gone, there was only one more connection to the plane and that was Steve. Nevertheless, in less than two hours, he too would be gone leaving no one left alive who had direct contact with that plane.

Queensbury, New York
Friday 11:19 p.m. (PST) - 1962

Giovanni was very concerned with the activities that had taken place at Vinchelli's and had just learned of Lou's death. He made a call to Anthony and told him to meet him at Sulleys in Queensbury. Sulleys was an old authentic Italian restaurant that was a safe haven for mob bosses to meet.

Anthony was a handsome man in his thirties. He had worked his way up through the ranks to become Giovanni's right hand man. Anthony would protect his boss at all costs. The money skimmed from the top of the New Jersey area waste management business receipts alone kept both men in a life of luxury. Anthony was not going to let anyone or anything cut into that action.

Anthony arrived dressed in a dark sports coat and slacks. His cream-colored shirt was unbuttoned to the chest. Around his neck, he wore a gold chain with a medallion that simply read *Trust and Honor.*

Anthony approached Giovanni sitting alone in the back of the restaurant.

"Hey G, what's up? Things good out West?"

Giovanni knew the situation they faced. It was unknown if the Feds really knew anything. Their mole, the Senator, was now in the morgue and Lou had just joined him there.

"I don't know Anthony. We've got some things we didn't count on."

"What are you talking about G?" Anthony asked.

"Well for starters, that Senator that fed us the information was dirty. He was working for the Feds all along. Lou swears he didn't tell him anything about the plans going down tonight, but I don't know. Seems Lou couldn't take it and decided to cash out tonight."

"No, don't tell me..." Anthony was shocked with what he was hearing.

Giovanni interrupted him, "I wish it wasn't true but we're in it up to here."

Giovanni brought his hand up to his neck illustrating his concerns. His facial features were one of disgust.

He continued, "We're going to have to do damage control. I sure am glad Jake had plans for doing away with the guys in charge of that plane."

Anthony was shocked about Lou.

"Aw Lou, why did ya have to go and do that?"

Giovanni was cold with his response.

"Lou did the right thing. Saved us from doing it. He should have been more careful. He brought it on himself."

"Have you talked with Jake yet about all this?" Anthony asked Giovanni.

"No...too late now. That plane is going to deliver in less than an hour. We are in this knee deep. Turning back now isn't even an option."

Both men finished a late meal and waited for word that all was well on the West Coast. They anxiously waited for the night's activities to conclude.

Above the Trinity National Forest, California
Friday 11:21 p.m. (PST) - 1962

The drone of the aircraft engine filled the cockpit with sound. Off in the distance Steve could see the California coast beginning to take shape.

His heart pounded with each second of the clock. He pointed the flashlight on the dash, familiarizing himself with one final look at all the controls. He needed to make sure he could reach and grab what was necessary because it was going to get busy in the cockpit very soon.

He could not get his mind off the strangeness of the missing *ST MPLS 62* initials he had seen carved into the dash when he first climbed aboard the plane. He had been watching the cockpit dash for a few hours now but the missing initials was creating an idiosyncrasy in his mind that did not add up. He questioned why the cockpit dash was now smooth where the etchings used to be. Steve wondered if it had any connection to the peculiar situation he faced.

His questions would have to be answered later. He was closing in on Eureka Airport and action was going to start soon.

Steve slowed the aircraft to near stall speed as he approached the Eureka Airport. His instructions were to arrive exactly at 11:30 p.m. Currently it was only 11:23 and he was only a few miles from the airport.

He thought about what to do. If he was early, would it cause his perpetrators to abandon their plans and blow the plane? If he turned to circle outside of the airport airspace, would they think he was on the run?

Steve finally decided to make a swooping turn to the right to bleed off some airtime. He thought whoever might be on the ground at the airport would not be able to identify the plane with the distance he was from the airport.

At exactly 11:28 p.m., Steve turned the aircraft toward Runway 33 and hit the throttle to maximum power. In a steep dive and at full power he planned to strafe the airport. He needed the airspeed should the plane engine not re-fire instantly when he flipped the magneto off and on.

The altimeter read 200 feet. The airspeed was pegged at 275 miles per hour as the aircraft reached the approach apron.

Eureka Airport, California
Friday 11:23 p.m. (PST) - 1962

Samantha sat at the end of the runway in the pickup truck waiting for the gold-laden plane to fly overhead. She seemed to glance at her watch every minute watching them tick away. Soon the entire plan would be in action and in a few short hours, her part would be done.

She did not know what she was going to do once the plan was complete. She rubbed her stomach and thought of the child she was carrying. She wondered if it were a boy or a girl.

She thought about her predicament. *How could she let herself get so involved with these thugs?* Ever since she was a child, she let adventure lead her into bad situations.

She so desired to return to the life she once knew with her husband and their white picket fence life. Her husband was so sweet. He trusted her with his entire being. Never did he think she was involved with the extortion racket that so wrapped up her life.

In the distance, she heard the drone of a plane but it seemed to turn away from the airport.

Must have been a pilot headed somewhere else, she thought.

She picked up the binoculars and scanned the sky looking for that payoff…the payoff that she secretly hoped would take her from the sordid life she had been living.

The flare gun sitting next to her was the signal to the American and Russian ships anchored off the California coast that the drop was underway. It sat ready to be fired the moment the plane was spotted.

Pacific Ocean - Sugarloaf Island
Friday 11:24 p.m. (PST) - 1962

The American boat bobbed up and down in the ocean waves. Don Carlo sat by the wheelhouse with his binoculars close at hand. The radio was tuned to Samantha's frequency and he waited to hear the words that the aircraft was on the way. He patiently waited to see the flare gun signal.

He wondered what twenty-five bricks of gold looked like. The amount of money it represented was staggering in his mind. He could not imagine spending that kind of money to have someone whacked, even if it was the President of the United States.

Little Al was getting antsy. He did not like to be confined and the American boat seemed to be getting smaller by the minute. He wanted this over and over now. He paced back and forth smoking cigarette after cigarette hoping to ease his tension.

His automatic rifle sat nearby. His trigger finger was itchy and he decided he had better lay the weapon down before he got trigger happy and started shooting at the rocks on the nearby island.

Vinnie sat on the stern watching the ocean water lap the side of the boat. He thought of Samantha's remarks while in the Eureka Harbor. He wondered if she would run. He hoped she wouldn't. He had grown close to her and hated to see her in such turmoil. He considered Samantha a good friend.

He worried about what her decision might be, but he worried more about what his employers would do if they caught her. She would not be able to hide. She would not be able to go back to her normal life. Once you are in the family, the only way out is by a coffin.

He determined that once this was over he was going to talk to her. Maybe he would be able to convince her that running was a bad idea. He had a soft spot in his heart for her and wanted to make sure she remained alive and safe.

Pacific Ocean - California Coast
Friday 11:25 p.m. (PST) - 1962

Krill, Stanislav, and Mikhail stood on deck of the Russian trawler waiting to see the flare signal. A school of dolphins frolicked playfully around the boat entertaining the men.

"Krill, if Americans double-cross, do we have plan?" Stanislav asked.

He wanted to know what was on the mind of his comrade. Stanislav was there for the ride and had no decision-making authority.

"Why must you think double-cross?" Krill angrily asked.

Mikhail joined in.

"We don't trust Americans. Maybe they work to trap us? Two golds is nothing for them to sacrifice. Maybe they draw us in and claim spy!"

Krill, recognizing the concern of his shipmates, backed off his angry responses to their questions.

"Okay, if Americans double-cross I have plan. Plan that stops Americans from talking. I will be ready to honor homeland. If Americans double-cross...no one will live. We will overcome any adversary."

Stanislav and Mikhail felt okay that Krill was not just thinking this was going to work. They were confident in his ability to deliver at all costs.

Eureka Airport, California
Friday 11:30 p.m. (PST) - 1962

Samantha was now standing outside of her pickup truck as Steve's plane approached. Her heart pounded. Secretively, she never thought this time would come. She figured someone would run off with the gold, if not the pilot himself.

Steve had the engine running maximum power as he quickly advanced on the Eureka Airport runway. He saw the pickup truck with a lone figure standing near the runway as he approached. He figured this must be another one of Billy's checkpoints.

Samantha quickly identified the approaching plane as the one carrying the gold. She did not wait for the plane to make the required low-level pass and climb to 2,000 feet. In her haste, she pointed the flare gun skyward and pulled the trigger.

The red trail of the flare gun charge spiraled high up into the air and flashed a brilliant white light as it exploded. The flash was seen by the American boat at Sugarloaf Island as well as the Russian boat waiting out in the Pacific.

Simultaneously, as Samantha fired the flare gun, Steve started his plan into motion. He quickly flipped the magneto off and on as he raced for the runway. The engine popped and sputtered, sending flames out the exhaust. He flipped the magneto to the on position and the engine re-fired much to Steve's relief.

He approached the mid-point of the runway and tried it again just as the flare exploded overhead. The aircraft crackled and popped as once again flames shot out the exhaust. The flare had illuminated the ground and it looked dangerously close.

Steve flipped the magneto to the on position...silence. The engine did not fire this time. Adrenaline pumped through Steve's veins. He tried it again. . .nothing! The airspeed was quickly bleeding off and the plane was dropping altitude; 200 feet, 175 feet, he snapped the switch back and forth wildly, 150 feet, 125 feet. Steve continued working the switch at 75 feet. He wondered if this was going to be the end?

Finally, at 50 feet the engine fired. Steve shoved the throttles to full power and as airspeed increased, so did the lift capacity of the wings. Steve once again had control of the plane.

Samantha was in a state of confusion. She wondered what had just happened. She heard the engine go silent but wondered why. *What was happening?*

She watched almost in panic as the plane started to glide downward toward the ocean. She had already fired the flare signaling the plan was in motion. If that plane crashes, would the Russians understand another delay? She breathed a sigh of relief when she heard the plane engine re-fire and saw it begin to gain altitude.

Steve did as he was told. He climbed to 2,000 feet to circle the airport. While circling he popped the magneto switch one more time. The engine had no problem firing this time.

Once he circled the airport, he killed the engine completely. He decided to dead-stick it onto the runway. With the misfires he caused while in the airport landing pattern, he thought the people on the ground would believe that the engine had completely failed. He hoped they would not trigger the bomb. He needed to get the plane on the ground in one piece.

Samantha heard the pop of the engine and then silence. She knew there was a problem. However, not only a problem with the plane, the entire operation was now compromised.

As she watched the plane circle and glide to the runway, she grabbed the two-way radio from her truck. The frequency was already tuned to the American boat. Samantha excitedly began calling to the American boat.

"Eureka to Sugarloaf! Eureka to Sugarloaf!"

"You got Sugarloaf. What's up over there? You sound excited, over."

"The plane is not going to make it. I repeat, the plane is not going to make it, over!"

"Eureka...you fired the flare. What the heck is going on, over?"

Samantha explained the predicament.

"I don't know Vinnie. The engine backfired a few times and then it just quit. It looks like the pilot is going to try to land this plane because he's lining up to the runway right now. The engine is not running."

Vinnie's voice turned solemn with the news of the plane. Vinnie did not waste any time. He told Don Carlo to pull the anchor and head for the Russian trawler at full speed.

Don Carlo started to question him.

"But we haven't..."

Vinnie did not let him finish his sentence.

"Never mind the questions right now. Just do it! I'll explain later."

Vinnie went back to the radio.

"Eureka, you guard that plane with your life. Do not let that pilot overpower you. You be ready with your gun the minute that canopy opens. But do-not-blow the plane. Do you understand? Do not blow the plane, over!"

"10-4 Vinnie. What are you going to do, over?"

"I'm going to go out and make peace with our friends off the coast. There isn't enough time to come in there, load the package, and get out to them. They saw the flare too and I just can't take a chance. I need to buy us a little more time to come ashore and then back out, over."

"Okay Vinnie. I'll guard this guy here but Vinnie...don't take too long, over."

"10-4, out."

Pacific Ocean - California Coast
Friday 11:31 p.m. (PST) - 1962

The light to the east was faint but unmistakable. Mikhail called to Krill.

"Krill, come look! Flare has been launched."

Krill came up from below. When he saw the light of the flare, a smile came to his face.

"You see, Americans follow their word okay. Gold will soon be in our hands. I tell you all would be good."

Stanislav, Mikhail, and Krill all laughed heartily. Soon the gold would be on board and all would be fine...or so they thought.

They waited patiently for the American ship to show on the horizon. They shared a few more shots of vodka as the faint light of a boat got brighter and closer. It was the American boat with Vinnie, Little Al, and Don Carlo at the helm.

Vinnie was going over exactly what he would tell Krill. He would explain what had happened...that the plane had engine failure. He would tell them that they would go to shore and retrieve the crate. They would then return to the Russian ship with the gold. It would be no big deal. . .just a little extra time.

The American boat parked alongside the Russian trawler as before. The three Russian faces were awash in smiles. They were expecting a huge payoff.

"So Mr. American, we finally have plan in place. You give me gold, we take your President."

Krill then let out another hearty laugh. The two other Russians chimed in. The laughter was short lived as Krill recognized the concern on Vinnie's face.

Krill climbed aboard the American boat and faced Vinnie with an evil stare.

"You look like something wrong. Where is woman?"

Vinnie replied to Krill's question.

"Oh we're all okay. Uh...Samantha...she's on shore in Eureka watching over things."

Vinnie swallowed hard.

"Well...listen Krill. We had a slight mishap. It seems our plane had an engine failure in Eureka. I came here right away to let you know. I didn't want to waste any time and have you wondering where we were. We're going to go back to the Eureka Airport and recover your gold and we'll have it right out to you. Okay?"

Krill looked back at Mikhail and Stanislav. He nodded to them and without warning, turned quickly, and slammed his fist squarely into Vinnie's jaw. The other two Russians quickly drew their weapons and trained them on Don Carlo and Little Al. The sudden actions took the American crew by surprise. They had no time to react in drawing their own weapons.

"Krill, we have the gold! Why are you doing this? We just need to change up the delivery plans a little. That's all. There is no need to worry," Vinnie pleaded.

Krill quickly snapped back.

"Shut up! You take us for fools? We wait and you Americans keep changing plans. We do not like change. We think you set us up."

Vinnie once again attempted to plead.

"No Krill...guys...listen..."

Krill again pummeled Vinnie with a left hook knocking him to the deck. He turned to his comrades and barked.

"Tie them up!"

Stanislav and Mikhail did as they were instructed. They stripped the three Americans of their weapons and tied each to the ship's deck.

Vinnie again pleaded.

"Listen Krill, you've got to believe me. Up in the wheelhouse is my radio that is in direct contact with Samantha who is at the Eureka Airport with the plane. Call her! See for yourself." Vinnie pleaded.

Krill would have no part in checking out Vinnie's story.

"You Americans think we fall in your trap? We will not allow this to happen. You double-cross and for that you pay."

Krill instructed his crew to find any excess gasoline they could find and spread it around the men tied to the deck. He also instructed his men to make sure the boats fuel tank openings were accessible and uninhibited.

Krill went to the wheelhouse and grabbed the radio Vinnie had told him was up there. He brought it down and propped it up in front of Vinnie. He keyed the radio-mic and taped it in the open position. Before turning the power on to the portable two-way radio, he looked Vinnie hard in the eyes and spoke to him in a menacing tone.

"Mr. Vinnie...Americans must learn not to play games with Russians. We are dangerous people. To show how dangerous, your comrades will hear your deaths."

Krill and his crew left the American boat and returned to the Russian ship. Before leaving, the last thing he did was turn the American's radio on. He wanted anyone who was listening to hear what he was about to do.

As the Russian trawler pulled away from the American boat, Vinnie immediately started calling out for Samantha. However, Samantha did not hear his immediate cries for help. She was facing her own crisis.

Eureka Airport, California
Friday 11:35 p.m. (PST) - 1962

The plane rolled to a silent stop. Steve had no clue what was going to happen next. He slide the canopy open and faced a young woman with a menacing looking pistol trained on him.

"Okay, I know this looks bad but I can't help an engine malfunctioning. You know I made all my checkpoints and then this happens. You must realize I can't fly a plane without an engine!"

Steve was pleading with the woman on the ground. He did not know her but he had a good idea who her employers were.

"Get out!" Samantha screamed at him.

Steve did as he was told and climbed from the plane. The sooner the better he thought. He knew he was sitting on a powder keg.

"What now?" Steve asked.

"You just never mind *what now.* You've cost us a lot of time and someone is going to pay for it!"

Steve, wanting to get away from the plane because of the explosives pleaded, "I realize you are holding the gun and I'm not going to do anything stupid, but do you mind if I walk around a little bit? That plane is not the best for pilot comfort and it sure would help to get the blood flowing again."

Samantha reluctantly agreed. She knew the plane was rigged with explosives and the timer was set to blow at 11:52 p.m. She was quickly trying to devise a plan to get the gold out and away from the plane in the 18 minutes she had left before the explosion.

"Walk slowly over to my truck," Samantha barked."

Steve did as he was instructed while Samantha kept her gun trained on him. Although he did not want the gold to go up in the explosion, he was glad to be away from the explosives himself.

Samantha and Steve reached the truck only to hear the cries of help on her two-way radio.

"Samantha…Samantha! Help! Are you there? You need to do something. The Russians think we double-crossed them. They think there is no gold! They've tied us to the deck. Gas is spread all over the place. Samantha...please!"

Vinnie's voice was beginning to crack. In the background she could hear the engine of another boat pulling away. Vinnie continued even louder.

"No...no...no! Samantha! Krill has a flare gun. It's pointed at us. Oh no! No! Samant...."

The radio went silent. The flash of a huge explosion off the coast could be seen from the airport. It took several seconds for the sound to reach Steve and Samantha and it sounded like distant thunder.

The Russian trawler steamed off to the west. The deal was over for them. Krill had made good on his promise of someone hearing the crew's death.

Samantha picked up the radio-mic and screamed, "Vinnie! Vinnie... Vinnie!"

The radio remained silent. She threw the radio-mic down and yelled out to sea.

"You murdering..."

Her emotions took control and she could not finish the sentence. She fought the tears that trickled down her cheek. She just lost three good friends.

Samantha never got to tell the crew what was on her mind when she stepped off the boat in Eureka. She put it off and now it was too late. What hurt the most was Vinnie. He was always there for her and this time she failed him.

CHAPTER 10

Eureka Airport, California
Friday 11:43 p.m. (PST) - 1962

Steve watched as Samantha tried to gather her emotions. She was distraught over the death of her friends. Steve could not concern himself with her right now though. He tried to reason with her.

"Hey listen...Samantha? Right?"

"Yes, Samantha," she dejectedly answered.

"I get it that you just lost somebody and I'm not trying to be rude or anything, but we have only a few minutes to either clear the area or get the gold out.

"You see, I overheard about the plane being rigged to blow once I dropped the gold. So, if we don't do something quickly, that plane is going to explode and shrapnel will be flying everywhere. What are you going to do?"

Samantha was trying to process all that had happened in the last few minutes. She did not even hear Steve confess that he knew about the bomb on the plane.

The entire plan was now blown. The thing that the mob wanted most was to have JFK removed. The Russians were going to do it for a lot of gold but now they were out of the picture. She was stuck holding the bag with no one left to make a decision but her.

She figured once Jake and Billy found out their plan was a bust, she would be held accountable and that would ultimately lead to her death. She had thought about trying to leave the life of crime after this one job but Samantha demised she might as well start running now.

Billy was on his way to the airport and once he discovered the plan was foiled, there would not be any hope for her. She had to decide quickly. Time was running out.

"Okay, here's the deal," she told Steve.

"I want out of this life I have been living. I will have to hide because the people I work for have no time for traitors. The way I see it I have two choices; one, run with just the clothes on my back or two, run with a pot of gold. Either way I'm dead if they ever catch up to me. I'm going to take their gold with me. At least I will have something of value to hide with."

Steve was agitated with her rambling. He just wanted to get out of there. However, he also did not want to leave the gold behind and have it fall back into the hands of Jake and Billy. The explosion would tear the plane apart but not a solid gold brick. They would be scattered but yet salvageable.

"You want the gold for you, fine. I just don't want Billy to get his hands on it. We don't have much time. Let's just take it and get our butts out of here. Do you agree Samantha?"

Samantha agreed but she did not know if Steve knew the plane was wired.

“Agreed but there is something else I need to tell you. The bomb doors are rigged with explosives. The plan was two minutes after you opened those doors the plane would be blown to pieces. We would have our gold and there would be no trace of where it came from.”

Steve rubbed his chin as he answered Samantha.

“Yeah, as I said, I knew all about it. Billy didn’t know I knew, but I overheard the entire plan when Billy talked outside the motel room with one of your fellow thugs. I know all about the mob wanting to whack JFK but listen, we just have minutes left. Not enough time to unpack the gold and get out of here. So we are going to have to diffuse the bomb instead.”

“Think you can do that?” Samantha asked.

“Yeah, I think so. I need a screwdriver.”

Samantha rummaged around the truck and found an old rusty flathead behind the seat.

“Will this do?”

She held up the screwdriver to Steve.

“Better than nothing. Hand me that flashlight and the wire cutters too. Let’s move,” he said.

Steve climbed back into the plane. He had a hunch that the bomb was activated by a switch wired to the bomb lever.

Samantha followed him and looked over his shoulder as he worked quickly. She noticed the rugged appearance Steve had. His shoulders were broad and muscular. She wondered about him if it were a different time and place. She wondered what it would be like to be with such a man.

Steve unscrewed the panel that housed the control mechanism for the bomb doors. He set the screwdriver on the panel ledge and peered into the opening with the flashlight. Unfortunately, his hunch was incorrect. Not even a wire from underneath could be seen. He exited the cockpit and told Samantha to get in.

"This is really important Samantha."

Steve pointed to the bomb release lever.

"I'm going to crawl underneath and when I yell, I want you to pull that lever all the way to the back. This will open the doors but do not push the red lever. That lever is the one that will actually release the crate and we're not ready for that. Then I want you to start counting loudly to 120. That will let me know how many seconds I have left to diffuse this thing. You got it?"

Samantha just shook her head up and down indicating she understood.

Steve grabbed the flashlight and the wire cutters and dropped to the ground. He crawled underneath the plane. He carefully went over the entire hatch area looking for any other wires. Once those doors opened, he would only have 120 seconds to either succeed or die.

Samantha sat staring at the cockpit panel.

What a life, she thought to herself.

Not one of her loved ones had any clue as to where she was or what she was doing.

She picked up the screwdriver Steve left behind and scratched in the cockpit panel...*ST MPLS 62.* It stood for Samantha Thompson, Minneapolis, MN in 1962. It gave her a sense of hope. She thought if she did not make it, someone would invariably trace the initials back to her. She wondered if anyone would even care.

Steve was finally ready to begin. He stepped back from the bomb bay doors. Then with flashlight and wire cutters in hand, he called out to Samantha.

"Pull that lever!"

Samantha did as instructed and started counting loudly, "One... two...three...four..."

The bomb doors swung open with a thud. Steve peered into the cavity. There he saw the elusive crate that seemed to relentlessly follow him around. Behind and above the crate he saw the crude perch with the bomb attached to it.

Samantha continued counting. As she counted down the seconds, sweat bubbles appeared above her upper lip.

"Twenty...twenty-one...twenty-two..."

Steve worked his way up and around the crate. His mind was racing. He could hear Samantha counting off the seconds. He had to do a quick study of the bomb to determine how it was wired.

He saw the timer and the battery pack. A red wire wound its way down to the bomb bay doors. He figured this went to the trigger mechanism. Next, he saw a blue and yellow wire protruding from the battery into the timer. He had to determine which one to cut. Cutting the wrong one would instantly trigger the bomb.

Samantha continued counting.

"105...106...Hurry! 108...109!"

Steve had to make a decision. It was now or never. He placed the wire cutters on the yellow wire and pulled!

The wire snapped and then silence. He had done it. The bomb was diffused.

He called to Samantha, "I did it. We're good."

Samantha stopped counting and breathed a sigh of relief. She wiped the sweat from her upper lip and climbed out of the plane.

"That was close. You sure it isn't going to blow?"

"Positive."

Steve held out the battery for her to see and then tossed it off to the side. He turned his attention to off-loading the gold.

Samantha had more news for Steve.

"One more thing. Billy, who you undoubtedly met, is on his way here. He could show up at any minute."

Steve sighed again and sarcastically said.

"Oh boy...it just keeps getting better. Back your truck up to the plane. Let's get this gold and get out of here."

Samantha backed the pickup truck to the edge of the plane. Steve climbed up the side of the plane to release the crate from the bomb mechanism.

He leaned over the edge of the cockpit for the release lever and something caught his attention. There was the screwdriver lying on the floor. Right above it were fresh scratch marks *ST MPLS 62* etched in the dash. The mystery of where they had come from had been solved. Samantha placed the initials there. He was puzzled as to what she meant by them. Steve would have to ask her later. There were more pressing issues right now.

Steve released the bomb lever and the crate dropped to the tarmac. The parachute and raft did not deploy as Marty had planned. The crate had not fallen far enough to activate the trigger mechanism.

Steve stared intently at the crate.

Why is this thing showing up in my life? Who would have known it contained gold?

These were the questions buzzing through his brain about this crate. When Steve first saw it in his office many weeks earlier, he had no idea so much mystery would surround it.

The crate was much too heavy for the two of them to pick up. They would be forced to unload it brick by brick into the back of Samantha's truck. The lock that clasped the metal bands together was heavy and large. Steve knew he would need something large to break it.

Samantha had nothing large enough in her pickup to smash it open. The pickup truck tire iron was much too small. Steve saw a repair shed across the tarmac and ran over to it. The door was locked but he managed to force it open anyway.

Inside he found a long steel pry bar that would do the trick. He brought it back to the plane and went to work on the lock. Taking aim, Steve lined up the end of the bar with the lock. By stabbing at the lock, the steel bar would transfer its weight energy to just the tip of the bar and hopefully break the lock open. After several tries, it worked and the lock let loose of its grip.

Steve eagerly removed the clasp that held the lid on. Samantha stood over him as he removed the wooden top. Anticipation was high. He threw the lid aside ready to extract the gold.

Samantha gasped as the lid was removed. Steve just stood up and kicked the side of the crate in disgust. They discovered the crate was not filled with the gold they were expecting but was filled with sandbags!

"I can't believe this. I saw the gold in Jake's office this afternoon. They were willing to kill me over a crate of sand! Unbelievable!" Steve exclaimed.

Samantha was left almost speechless. She had a hard time fathoming someone would put her in such a compromising position. She thought of Vinnie and the boys. They had no clue they had been double-crossed and died for nothing.

Steve was going over in his head where the gold could have been taken. *Who pulled off the switch?* He thought of the players he had seen in the last few hours.

Earlier That Afternoon in the Motel Room
Friday 2:05 p.m. (PST) - 1962

Luke, driving the Lincoln Continental, brought Billy and Steve from the Cal Neva Casino to the motel room. Here Steve would wait out his time with Billy until it was flight time.

Steve was told to sit in the chair while Billy and the driver talked softly.

Billy whispered to Luke, "When you get to the airport, Tony and Marty should be gone. Marty thinks the plane has been rigged to blow should the bomb doors open, but Tony has left the wire to the trigger mechanism unattached. When you get there, make sure no one is around and make the switch; the sand for the gold. Tony left the key for the crate lock on top of the bomb.

"When you pull the gold out and replace it with the sand, be careful not to disturb the chute. We need this crate to go all the way to the Russians without the switch being noticed until it gets in their hands and they've opened it.

"Leave the gold in the trunk of the Lincoln and when we get to Trinidad, we'll each take our share. The suspension on the Lincoln is good enough to hold the weight. Remember, before closing the bomb doors make sure to connect the yellow wire to the battery to arm the bomb. Got it?"

"Sure thing boss," Luke responded.

"Oh and Luke, here's a few bucks. On your way back here later, get us some burgers or something to eat. We're going be hungry by the time you return."

The Eureka Airport, California
Saturday 12:10 a.m. (PST) - 1962

Steve played the scenario out in his mind. He thought of each individual he had met. First, there was Jake. Surly he wouldn't steal his own gold. No reason for that.

The only other person he had contact with was Billy. He was an individual that was cold and calculating. He also seemed to be a nervous individual. He was constantly smoking cigarettes.

Steve thought about the people that visited the motel earlier. Marty seemed to make Billy jittery and jumpy. He wondered why.

Could Billy be the one, Steve thought.

He asked Samantha her opinion on his theory.

"Samantha, do you think Billy could have been the one to do the double-cross and take the gold?"

She leaned against the pickup truck and looked at the stars as she answered.

"It really doesn't matter now. I was going to get out after this job anyway. My friends on the boat were to pick me up after they paid the Russian's their gold. After that we were going to head down the coast.

"I had determined I wasn't going to be here when they got back. I was planning to leave this life and try to resume a normal one. It wouldn't have been so bad had the gold been there. But now someone is going to be looking for blood with this gold disappearing act."

Steve asked again.

"That's fine Samantha on getting out, but I want to know who stole that gold. I cannot stand the thought of a U.S. President getting whacked because someone doesn't like what's going on or for any other reason for that matter. So I ask again, do you think Billy was the one who took the gold?"

"Walk with me," Samantha told him.

As they walked, she told Steve her thoughts on Billy.

"Billy, now he's a real work of art. If anyone is cold-hearted in this business, he is. I've seen him do some terrible stuff to people when he was working extortion for Jake. He is one vicious little man.

"Do I think he stole the gold? Yeah, my bets are on Billy. Someone that cold would sell his own mother's soul for a dime.

"As far as JFK getting whacked…well I was never much for politics anyway. I was just doing my job."

They continued walking without a direction in mind. They paused in front of the shed where Steve had found the bar to break the lock on the crate. Both looked back at the plane. Steve continued the conversation.

"What was the plan for everybody after the Russian's got the gold? Was everyone just going to hide out or what?"

"More or less." Samantha answered.

"Like I said, my crew and I were going to head down the coast and lay low in the San Francisco area. You know, wait for the heat to blow over.

"Billy, Frankie, Tony, Lester, and Luke were all going to meet at a restaurant up the coast in Trinidad. They had their own agenda. I'm not quite sure what it was.

"However, we were all told to lay low and not cause any unnecessary attention. Things were going to happen quickly."

"What do you mean *things*?" Steve asked.

"You know about the gold drop, the hit on JFK, and all that. But I'm not sure you know how it was going to work.

"The big boys out East didn't want to be tied in any way to something this huge. They wanted JFK out but wanted someone to be on the hot seat for it. Everyone had connections in this elaborate plan but it boiled down to the Russians doing the job.

"I had the contact with them. When you missed your deadline yesterday, I had to do some fast explaining to them. They were quite perturbed with the delay. Their people were already in place and ready to follow through on the hit. The only thing they were waiting on was the payoff in gold."

Steve was convinced that history was about to be changed. The Russians did not have the gold as far as Steve knew. Therefore, he assumed the assassination attempt on JFK would be stopped. However, with the gold missing he could not be positive. He would not rest until the gold was found.

"Listen Samantha, has the name Lee Harvey Oswald ever been mentioned?"

"Hmmm...no I can't say that I recognize that name. Who is that?"

Steve thought about what he asked Samantha. Should he continue and tell her the truth about him? Should he tell her he was from the future and not from her present day? Should he tell her President Kennedy was assassinated in '63?

He decided not to tell her anything right now. If the future presents an opportunity, then he would, but for now he just needed to find the gold.

He told her, "Oh nothing, just wondering. That name came up in my path and I wanted to see if you recognized it."

Samantha was getting anxious knowing that Billy was scheduled to stop by the airport. Billy had planned to meet with her and the boat crew before they left for the Coast. He needed to get the low down on the meeting with the Russians. With the turn of events, she now wondered what his real intentions were actually going to be.

Samantha looked back to the pickup truck parked near the plane. She thought they had better leave before Billy showed.

"Well listen, if I am going to make it alive, I've got to get out of here. Can I drop you anywhere?"

Steve thought about taking her up on the offer but declined since he had the plane. Without the thing rigged to explode, he was okay. He was on a quest to find that gold and the plane would give him the transportation he needed.

Samantha and Steve were about to walk back to her pickup truck and the plane when they saw headlights coming through the trees. Both were not sure who it was but had a fairly good idea it was Billy.

The vehicle quickly approached the area. Samantha and Steve were out in the open.

"No time to run. Quick, duck back in the shed," Steve told Samantha.

Both got inside just as the car rounded the corner to the where the plane and pickup truck were parked. The car crawled to a stop a mere thirty feet from where Samantha and Steve were hiding. They crept to a dusty window to peer out and see if their hunch was correct.

The person driving the car sat behind the wheel for several moments before stepping out. Samantha and Steve watched as the car door opened. The person stepped out of the car and stood on the tarmac. It was Billy!

Steve and Samantha's hearts pounded as they watched him move from the car to the pickup truck. As he approached the vehicle, he pulled his gun from inside his jacket. The light glimmered off the chrome-plated weapon.

As he peered into the pickup truck, a second vehicle approached. It stopped next to Billy's car. Steve recognized the individual driving as Frankie.

"Billy, what gives man? I thought this plane was to be in a million pieces over the ocean floor by now?"

Billy was just as confused as Frankie.

"I don't know Frankie. I don't know! I just rolled up myself. Something isn't right here."

Frankie retrieved a flashlight from his front seat. Both he and Billy walked toward the plane. As they approached the open crate sitting on the ground next to the plane, Frankie clicked on the flashlight and focused the beam on the object.

"What the…it's sand Billy. It's a box of sand!"

Billy was confused and irritated at the same time. This box of sand was to be in the Russians hands creating numerous questions and problems for his bosses. The plane and its pilot were to have been blown apart. However, here they both were and no sign of the pilot or Samantha.

Billy grabbed the flashlight and crawled under the plane as he answered Frankie.

"Again Frankie, I don't know. I am as confused as you are. Look, there's the bomb. It never went off!"

"Well duh…Billy. The plane is still sitting here. This is not good. I need to find a phone and call this into Jake. This is really bad."

Frankie had no clue as to the plans by Billy, Tony, and Luke to steal the gold right out from under the mob and the Russians. It was an audacious plan that the three thought they could pull off.

Samantha and Steve continued hiding in the shed listening to the conversation the two men were having. As they peered from the bottom of the shed window, both were unprepared for what happened next.

Billy crawled out from under the plane while Frankie headed for his car to find a phone. He had no idea what was going on behind him. Billy stopped and raised his gun.

He simply said, "Aw, Frankie, Frankie, Frankie."

Before the man could turn around Billy pulled the trigger and shot Frankie in the back. Frankie was dead before his head bounced off the pavement.

Billy looked around to see if anyone saw what had happened. He quickly realized he was a bit careless in his actions.

He walked over to Samantha's pickup truck and peered in again. He saw Samantha's two-way portable radio. He pulled it out, turned it on, and keyed the radio-mic.

"Central to Don Carlo, over."

The sound of static was all that could be heard. He tried again.

"Central to Don Carlo…Samantha come in, over."

Again, the radio was nothing but static.

Billy fumbled with the radio until he dialed in the frequency for the harbor Coast Guard. He made a fictitious radio call.

"Eureka Harbor Coast Guard. This is November Charlie 312, come in please."

"November Charlie 312, this is Coast Guard. Go ahead, over."

"Hey listen, me and some buddies were going on a night cruise and I was late getting here. They were returning to the harbor to pick me up about an hour ago. Can you tell me if anyone has arrived in the last hour or so, over?"

"Negative November Charlie 312. But we did have a vessel explode and sink off the coast several miles out about an hour ago. Search and rescue is working on that now, over."

"10-4, November Charlie 312, out."

"Eureka Harbor Coast Guard, out."

Billy threw the radio in disgust. He felt the front of the engine on the pickup truck. He did the same to the plane's engine. Both were warm. Billy knew he had not missed Steve and Samantha by very much time.

Billy began to look around. He walked toward the shed where Steve and Samantha were hiding. Both quickly dropped to the floor and held their bodies against the wall.

Billy approached the shed's window. He wiped the dust from the pane and peered in. Steve and Samantha could see the silhouette of his body in the shadow on the floor. After a few minutes he walked back to the plane. Steve and Samantha again gingerly peered out the window.

They watched Billy as he walked up to the plane. Both could tell he was disgusted as he kicked the wooden crate of sand. All of a sudden, he twirled toward the plane, pulled his gun again, and fired several rounds at the plane in a rage. He then got into his car, threw it in gear, and squealed the tires as he left.

Steve and Samantha cautiously left their hiding place. Steam was rising from the body of Frankie as they walked past it on their way to where the plane and Samantha's pickup truck were parked.

Steve examined the plane for damage left by Billy's gun. The oil cooler had a couple of bullet holes in it rendering the plane useless.

"Well this plane is shot for flying. Samantha, would you mind giving me that ride now?"

"If you want one, let's go. I've had enough of this place."

Steve and Samantha jumped in the pickup truck and drove away from the airport. She was leaving behind memories of good friends lost to unscrupulous killers. Steve was leaving behind the plane that brought him to another dimension. He wondered how or if ever he would get back to reality.

CHAPTER 11

Highway 101, California
Saturday 1:33 a.m. (PST) - 1962

The night air was cool as Samantha and Steve left the airport. She asked Steve where he wanted to go.

Steve answered, "Well I have to follow the gold trail and I believe that takes me to Trinidad about 25 miles up the road. That is if your information was correct."

Samantha questioned him and his motives.

"Why? Why would you put yourself in danger like that? You're just a pilot. Don't be some hero over this. It's not worth it."

"Samantha, yes I am just a pilot but there is so much more you don't understand."

Steve again contemplated telling her the complete story. His instincts told him not to. He decided to explain his immediate motives only.

"I've seen a lot in this world. More than you can really understand. Life is too precious to be lost in the world of greed. Where Billy is…is a bad place. He will end up paying dearly for the actions he has chosen in life. I mean, we just saw him waste another human being just because he had his own agenda. How cold can you be to do that?

"What about you Samantha? What's your motive for running?"

Steve could not see it but a tear rolled from Samantha's eye and dripped from her chin.

"My motive…I'm pregnant. I have a husband that loves me. He has no idea what I have gotten myself involved with.

"These past few years have been a lie. I chased adventure and it has cost me. I'm not sure I can face my husband for what years I have left with him and still hide what I have done. I just have to head back home to Minneapolis and pick up the pieces of my life. Hopefully I will still have enough pieces left."

Steve said nothing more. He knew she was right. The secrets she kept from her husband would haunt her for life. She could not change the past. She could not undo the choices she had made. They were engraved in her being.

Steve contemplated what his next move would be while Samantha cried silently as she drove toward the California coastal town of Trinidad.

Highway 101, California
(Several miles ahead of Samantha and Steve)
Saturday 1:33 a.m. (PST) - 1962

Billy thought about his next move. Jake no doubt would find out about the missing gold. He had to come up with a plan before Jake discovered the truth and ended up taking his anger for the misfortune out on him.

His mind raced as if it were on a road with no end. He had so many loose ends to clean up. Luke was on his way to Trinidad and would arrive soon. He had no clue that Billy had killed two of their partners; Tony in the backwoods on the way to Eureka and Frankie at the airport. Billy wondered how Luke would take the news that Tony and Frankie were both dead.

Lester was another source of concern. Tony was the one that had the task of eliminating him. With Tony dead, Billy had to re-think a new plan to cover his tracks with Lester. That left only one alternative. Billy would have to make Lester another casualty of greed.

He also needed a story to tell Luke about Tony. Billy figured he would tell him that Tony was getting cold feet about stealing the gold and had to be eliminated.

Next, he wondered where Samantha and Steve were.

Did they just run and hide? How did Steve land the plane without it blowing up? And the bomb doors...why were they open without the entire place being blown to bits?

Billy had many questions all right! Questions that may have clouded his judgment for the decisions he would make in the near future. Greed would soon be his all consuming quest.

Sea-Surf Restaurant - Trinidad, California
Saturday 2:00 a.m. (PST) - 1962

Billy pulled into the parking lot of the Sea-Surf Restaurant in Trinidad, California. The restaurant was built on a cliff high above the crashing Pacific Ocean. Rocks scattered the surf below. He was the first to arrive.

It was late and long past the restaurant's closing time but the balcony overlooking the surf was accessible. He stood watching the wave's crash one after another on the rocks below. Soon the others would arrive and he would have to come up with a plan. A plan that was not only workable but also believable.

Billy decided he would take a chance and call Jake. He had an idea that just might work. It was worth a try. He was out of options.

Billy walked to a pay phone on the opposite end of the balcony. He dialed zero for the operator to make a collect call.

"May I help you?" the operator answered.

Billy told her he wanted to make a collect call to the Cal Neva Casino. The call went through and Jake accepted the charges.

"Hey Billy boy, I've been waiting to hear from you. Everything go as planned?"

"Boss, got some really bad news."

Jake was leaning back in his office chair with a cigar between his lips. He immediately sat up straight and stuffed the lit cigar in the ashtray on his desk. His eyebrows furrowed as he spoke.

"What do you mean bad news?"

"We all did our job boss. The plane was rigged. The gold was loaded. That pilot made every checkpoint. But something happened in Eureka."

Jake interrupted, "The Russians got their gold, right?"

"No boss, that's what I'm trying to tell you. I got to the Eureka Airport and Samantha's pickup truck was there with the plane. For some reason the plane landed in Eureka without blowing up. I think I interrupted Samantha and that pilot stealing the gold. The wooden crate was there but the gold wasn't."

Jake seethed with anger.

"Did you find those two and if you did...bring them to me at once? They will wish they had never seen the day they were born!"

"No Jake. I didn't find them. In fact, the gold was gone too."

"Why I will—," Billy interrupted Jake.

"But wait there is more bad news. They shot Frankie."

"I can't believe this. We put so much planning in this and it all went south. Billy, I want you to find those two and bring them to me. I don't care how you do it…just get it done!"

Billy hung up the phone. His confidence was riding high in his performance to Jake. He decided not tell Jake just yet about Tony. He needed to work up an alibi regarding his death.

He lit a cigarette and waited for Luke and Lester to show up in Trinidad. Lester had no clue he would never leave the coastal town.

Trinidad, California
Saturday 2:05 a.m. (PST) - 1962

Samantha pulled to the back of a service station on the outskirts of town. The only road leading into Trinidad was void of traffic that night. She parked her pickup out of sight but in a way that had a clear view of anyone coming into town. She and Steve knew Billy was there but not his exact location.

Steve had convinced Samantha to wait just a few minutes so he could follow Luke or Lester to where Billy was. After that, she was free to go wherever it was she needed to run.

"Hey listen Samantha, I truly am sorry you lost some good friends tonight. I appreciate that you understand I need to pursue this to the end. Thanks for helping me out."

"You know, I've done a lot of bad things in the last few years. The insanity had to stop. I couldn't just walk out on you as I walked out on so many other people these past few years. In a few minutes, you will go your way and I will go mine. But if you are ever in the Minneapolis area…look me up…Samantha Thompson. I won't be running anymore."

Again, Steve contemplated being honest with her about who he really was and where he was from. However, the time was not right to go into it and he was not sure she would believe him anyway.

He simply said, “I will.”

The headlights of a car could be seen coming down the road. As it approached, the street lamp near the gas station where Samantha and Steve were hidden illuminated the inside of the approaching car. They recognized the driver as Lester.

Steve looked to see if there were any other cars around. There was not.

“Follow him.” Steve told Samantha.

Samantha followed Lester’s car at a distance with her headlights off. They saw him stop at the Sea-Surf Restaurant.

“I should have known.” Samantha said.

“What’s that?” Steve asked.

“Back a few weeks when these plans were in motion Billy asked me if I had ever eaten at the Sea-Surf Restaurant. I told him no but I had heard great things about it. He said if he ever got in the area, he would try it out. Looks like he’s a little late to try today’s special.”

Steve smirked, “Yeah, I think so. Well Samantha, good luck on your journey. I’ll get out now and let you be on your way. I think I can handle things myself from here.”

Samantha smiled and leaned over and gave Steve a hug. It took Steve by surprise. He had a deep sense that this would not be the last he would see or hear of her.

Steve jumped out in the darkness and headed down the opposite side of the restaurant away from where Billy and Lester were. Samantha drove off in her pickup truck. He wondered if she would ever make Minneapolis before the mob caught up to her.

Lester parked his car next to Billy’s and walked out onto the balcony to greet Billy.

"Hey Billy. We did it man! We actually pulled this thing off."

He looked around for the other guys.

"Where's Tony, Frankie, and Luke? Don't tell me I beat these guys here? I came all the way from Grass Valley for God's sake and look what that hotshot pilot did to my shirt with that circus stunt of buzzing me with the plane."

Lester pointed to the coffee stains down the front of himself.

"Yeah Lester you beat the others here. Frankie is with Tony in Eureka. They waited with Samantha until the boat picked her back up. Anybody follow you in?"

"No one Billy. This place is so desolate I don't think the coyotes are even awake."

Billy lit a cigarette and offered one to Lester. He declined. The two men made small talk while they waited for Luke. Lester had no clue Tony and Frankie would never arrive.

Steve peeked around the corner and watched the men as they talked. He wondered what was going to happen. They were just standing there leaning on the rail of the balcony high above the surf.

A car could be heard coming down the gravel drive. The tires of the vehicle made a crunching sound as it ran over the stones in the driveway.

The huge car stopped next to Lester's vehicle. It was the same Lincoln that brought Steve to the motel earlier.

Luke stepped from the car. Billy left Lester on the balcony and walked toward the parking lot. He met Luke halfway down the walkway.

"Hey Luke, we need to talk a minute. I don't want Lester to hear us. First, the plane is sitting on the ground at the Eureka Airport."

"What!"

"Yeah, Samantha's truck was there too. I didn't see her or the pilot. I don't know what is going on here.

"One more thing, Tony and Frankie are both dead. I had to shoot Tony a few hours ago on the way to Eureka when he pulled a gun on me. I think he had plans of his own.

At the airport, Frankie tried to make a dash for a phone to call Jake about the plane. As you can understand, I couldn't let that happen until I figured out what was going on myself."

Luke asked, "Lester know?"

"No, I didn't say anything. I didn't want to spook him."

Luke just sighed and said, "Well let's get this done. We'll talk more later."

Both men returned to Lester on the balcony. The three of them talked for a few moments but Steve could only hear bits and pieces of their voices and could not make out any discerning conversation.

He was scoping out a closer location to the three when the scuffle broke out. Lester came crashing to the floor of the balcony with Billy on top of him. Lester was lying flat on his back with Luke struggling to hold Lester's arms up and away from his body. Billy pulled out his gun and pistol-whipped Lester repeatedly over the head.

The beating was so severe that it was just a few moments before Lester lay motionless. Billy stood up and put his gun back in his holster. Luke and Billy stood conversing with each other for a few minutes. Luke pointed toward Lester's car.

Steve saw the two men carry Lester's limp body to his car. They threw him to the ground next to the curb. Next Luke got in Lester's car and realigned it so it faced the balcony of the restaurant. The downward incline led directly to the wooden railing.

Billy and Luke positioned Lester's unconscious and bleeding body in the driver's seat. Billy reached through the window, started the car, and pulled the gearshift into drive.

The car slowly crept forward but gained momentum as it rolled down the incline. By the time the car reached the railing it was going fast enough to break through the barrier with ease.

Steve watched in horror as the rear of the car dropped out of sight over the busted railing. Moments later he heard a crash and an explosion as the car ripped itself apart on the rocks below.

Steve was not sure if Lester perished without knowing what had transpired thus far. He went to his death without the ability to fight for his life.

Steve started deriving a conclusion regarding the people he had contact with during the last several hours.

First, there was Marty. He heard the phone call earlier between Jake and Billy but by the end of the conversation Steve could tell Marty would not live through the day.

Next, there was Frankie. Steve saw him get shot in the back at the Eureka Airport. A cold-blooded murder perpetrated at the hands of Billy.

Now Lester was murdered by Luke and Billy. Steve witnessed him beaten unconscious and then sent over the cliff to a certain death. The crash on the rocks below would certainly cover any marks left by the beating.

Then there was Samantha's crew. He heard their deaths by explosion at sea over Samantha's radio.

That left four players alive that he was aware of. First, there was Jake. Steve counted him out because undoubtedly he would not steal his own gold. Then Billy and Luke were right there in plain sight. However, Tony was still missing. Steve had no clue where he was.

He thought that maybe Billy and Luke were waiting for him to show up. His theory was soon short lived when he saw Billy and Luke climb in the Lincoln.

They started the car and headed down the driveway. The gravel drive was riddled with potholes. Steve had been around machinery all his life and thought it very odd the suspension on the Lincoln made very little movement as it traversed the potholes.

He was watching the two men leaving when the picture started becoming clearer. Steve remembered back in the motel room Billy whispering to Luke and then giving him a few bucks which appeared to be for food. Luke returned with burgers and fries. They were good and they were warm as if they were just cooked. However, Luke left around 2:30 p.m. and did not return until after 6:00 p.m. Steve wondered where he was for almost four hours.

Shortly after Luke left, Marty showed up at the motel. Steve remembered the conversation Billy had with Marty outside the room. Marty was worried about the plan to assassinate the President going off without a hitch. Billy tried to reassure him all was fine but also wanted to make sure the gold was in the plane and it was rigged to blow.

As soon as Marty left the motel, Billy called and cast doubt with Jake regarding Marty's nerves. Soon afterwards, Marty was whacked.

Steve watched the Lincoln drive further away. Then it hit him. He muttered aloud to himself.

"It's the Lincoln. The gold is in the Lincoln! That's why there was no suspension travel on the big car. Billy was the mastermind of the entire operation to steal the gold!"

Now the gold was leaving the area in the back of the Lincoln and Steve was left standing in the drive. Initially, Steve chased after the car on foot by instinct but there was no way for him to keep up. He had to find a way to follow these men.

Steve saw Billy's car still in the parking lot and raced to it. He kept his eye on the receding taillights of the Lincoln and his two suspects.

"Agh…no keys!"

Steve reached under the dash and felt around for the ignition wires. Since he grew up on a farm, he was very good at hot-wiring vehicles that had no keys. His training helped and within a few seconds, the car engine roared to life.

Steve threw the car into gear and spewed gravel as he sped out of the parking lot in his quest to catch up to the Lincoln. Steve was cautious in following the Lincoln. He did not want the two men he was following to become wise that they had a tail.

Just outside of Trinidad, California
Saturday 2:20 a.m. (PST) - 1962

Luke and Billy headed for the Eureka Airport. Billy thought it would be good to get the empty crate to show Jake. There also was the matter of Frankie's body to dispose of. Billy left in haste and should have done the job when he was there. Now they had to back track to clean up the mess.

Steve followed at a distance. He was not aware of the headlights far behind him. His concern was the car in front of him. He needed to follow his hunch that the gold was in the trunk of that Lincoln.

Luke was not the trusting person Billy thought him to be. In addition, Billy was not above rubbing Luke out and taking the gold for himself. Luke broached the subject first.

"Hey Billy, just to make sure we understand each other, I don't trust you. Plain and simple, I don't trust you. Tony, Frankie, and Lester did and look where it got them."

"Come on Luke, you don't have to worry."

"I know I don't have to worry. I've taken care of that," Luke responded.

"And to make sure, if anything should happen to me, a letter will be presented for everyone to see. A letter that explains everything and naming names that would bring down a lot of heat from oh so many directions. So much heat you wouldn't be able to hide anywhere."

Billy just sat there and stared out the window watching the telephone poles whizzing by.

Earlier - Grass Valley, California
Friday 10:00 p.m. (PST) - 1962

Earlier that evening, Luke had parked at the end of Runway 25 at the Nevada County Airport with his two-way radio turned off. He knew Steve would not be flying over for a little while and he wanted the time to himself to reflect on the day's activities. He did not want to hear the radio clutter between the other checkpoints.

Hours earlier, under the direction of Billy, he had ripped off the mob by stealing the gold out of the plane Steve was going to be flying. It was a bold move. If caught, it would mean certain death for him and his family.

The pressure was almost too much to bear. Just a few feet from him in the trunk of his car was twenty-five gleaming gold bricks worth a fortune…a fortune that was supposed to go to the Russians to assassinate the President of the United States!

There were many players in on this one. If this worked, Billy, Tony and he would be very rich men but also very sought after by some ruthless characters.

Billy and Tony convinced Luke they could do this and that it would be simple and clean. By dropping sand for the Russians to receive rather than the gold, it would infuriate them so much the mob bosses would not be safe anywhere they went. This in turn would keep the heat off them until the coast was clear to fence the gold.

However, Luke was still unsure. Too many things had to happen at once to pull this off. Besides, he never did trust Billy and he knew Tony would do anything Billy instructed.

Luke pulled out a pad of paper and wrote two letters. One was to go to his brother and the other to a close family friend. In the letters he explained who did what to whom and why. He sealed each one in an envelope and wrote instructions on the outside not to open unless Luke met with his demise or disappeared. He then placed each in an outer envelope and dropped them in a mail slot at the airport.

Luke was not taking any chances. If Billy wanted to knock him off, Luke was going to get the last laugh by exposing Billy's plan.

After this little task, Luke turned the two-way radio back on and settled in to wait for the plane to make a low-level pass carrying nothing but a crate of sand and a bomb.

Eureka Airport, California
Saturday 3:05 a.m. (PST) - 1962

Luke and Billy pulled into the Eureka Airport and headed to where the plane was parked. Steve had followed close behind and as he approached the airport he turned off his headlights.

The headlights of the Lincoln illuminated the carnage around the plane. The plane sat in the same place where Steve had left it. The bomb bay doors were swung wide open and the crate of sand sitting below them.

There was Frankie's car right where he had parked it. Next to it laid the body of Frankie with a couple of bullet holes in his back. All looked the same as when Billy bolted earlier.

However, what startled Billy was the fact that Samantha's pickup truck was gone. He relayed his concern to Luke.

"Luke, when I left, Samantha's pickup truck was here. It was right there and now it's gone!"

Billy pointed to an area near the plane.

"Son of a…they must have been here the entire time I was…. Agh…I should have done a better search of the area. I should know better."

Billy had a sick feeling in the pit of his stomach. He wondered if Steve and Samantha had seen him shoot Frankie in the back.

Luke said, "Let's get this done and get out of here. This place gives me the creeps."

Steve watched from a distance as the two men picked up the body of Frankie and propped him up in the driver's seat of his car. Luke positioned the car so it was heading straight down the runway. He tied the steering wheel with a piece of wire he ripped from the plane.

Next, he started the car and placed it in drive with a sandbag on the accelerator. The car acted just as expected. It gathered momentum down the runway. The plan was to have it run off the edge of the runway and fall off into the ocean but instead the car hung up on the huge rocks at the end of the runway. The wheels were still spinning but were not making traction with any ground to continue the car moving forward.

Luke and Billy knew they could not just leave the car with Frankie's body sitting there. They had to get rid of it.

Luke said, "I know what we can do."

Luke went back to the Lincoln and pulled out the bomb trigger mechanism he had with him. He set it on the car's hood. He then climbed under the plane and up into the bomb well. He carefully removed the explosives from inside the plane. However, he realized the battery pack was missing.

"Billy, look for a battery pack. Without it, this bomb is not going to work."

Luke and Billy searched around the area looking for the small device about half the size of a car battery. After a few minutes, Billy called out.

"Here it is!"

Billy handed the battery pack over to Luke.

"Great. Now let's create a little 4th of July of our own with Frankie as the star attraction," Luke smirked.

Both men walked to where the car was perched on the rocks. The car's engine was still racing. Luke reached in and turned the car off.

"No need to waste gas." Luke chuckled.

Billy smirked as he set the bomb he had been carrying on Frankie's lap.

"Here ya go Frankie. Just a little going away present for you," Billy said mockingly.

Nothing was going to be left when that bomb went off. Billy only wished the original plan had worked and it was Steve and the plane that was going up in pieces.

The men returned to the plane. They took the sand bags out of the crate and placed the empty wooden crate in the backseat. They threw one of the sandbags in the crate for good measure. Luke then grabbed the bomb trigger from the car hood and both men climbed back into the Lincoln.

Luke held the trigger mechanism.

He smiled and said, "Frankie my boy...have a good flight."

He pushed the button and a huge explosive fireball shot skyward. The explosion was massive and totally disintegrated the car.

Luke and Billy left the airport in a hurry. Their work was done. Steve followed them at a safe distance out to the highway. He was looking for the right opportunity to catch the two thieves by surprise.

Fortuna, California
Saturday 4:10 a.m. (PST) - 1962

Luke and Billy pulled into the small motel just outside of town. It had been a very long evening and rest was in order. Steve too was feeling the effects of a long night, but he fought the fatigue.

The motel was off the beaten path so it had very few guests. Billy requested the room at the end of the one story building. Luke parked the big Lincoln just outside the door of their room.

"I don't know Luke, think the car will be okay here? There's a lot of money in the trunk."

"Billy, I'm tired. The gold will be fine. I've been all over this state with that stuff in the trunk since yesterday and nothing has happened so far. Let's just get some sleep. We've got to face Jake tomorrow and make it stick that the pilot and Samantha made off with the gold."

"I suppose you're right Luke. But I'm not going to sleep very well knowing I'm in there and the gold is out here in the parking lot."

Steve had pulled in around the corner and out of sight. He parked so he could watch the two men. They went into the motel room and it was not too long before the lights went out.

Steve fought the urge to sleep. He had been up for almost 24 hours now but he resisted the temptation to nap. He had a mission to complete.

After thirty minutes, he was sure the two goons were fast asleep. The parking lot and motel office were also quiet.

He thought long and hard as to where Billy and Luke might be taking the gold. He tried to figure out if they were going to run with it or hide it somewhere.

Steve discounted the thought of the two men running. The mob has many connections and somewhere, no matter where they might try to run, eventually the mob was going to find them.

He thought about the empty crate and why they brought it with them. He understood their need to get rid of Frankie, but the crate was puzzling Steve. He thought there must have been a reason they wanted to keep the empty crate but what was it?

Then Steve remembered the phone call Billy made in Trinidad just before Lester and Luke arrived. He sounded like he was talking to someone in authority. Billy was pushing the blame toward Samantha and Steve.

Then it struck him. If Billy and Luke could make the story stick that the gold was stolen by Samantha and Steve, it would keep the heat off them. Eventually, the two of them could cash in on the gold and no one would be the wiser.

Steve had other plans. He was not going to stand for those two getting away with murder and bringing heat down on someone else. He determined he would put an end to this by taking the gold himself and exposing these two crooks.

Steve slowly slipped out of the car. He looked underneath the car to examine the suspension. It looked fairly stout. The gold was heavy but the car should hold up.

Next, he needed to pop the trunk on the Lincoln. He looked all through the car and the only thing he could find was a piece of wire like a coat hanger. He knew he would only have one shot at this.

Steve crept ever so quietly to the rear of the Lincoln. He looked from side to side and saw no one. The lights were out in Billy and Luke's motel room. He crept slowly up to the driver's door, slid the wire through the wing window, and pulled back on the locking mechanism.

He was in luck. The locking bar had not been pushed down tight where as the lock button would hold it in place.

Steve pulled back on the bar, opening the wing window. He reached inside and opened the driver's door to gain access to the vehicle. He entered the car and gently shut the driver's door. He then climbed into the back seat where the wooden crate was sitting.

Seeing the crate gave Steve an eerie feeling. Here he was staring at the same crate that had been so prevalent in his life and now it was up close again. Close enough he could smell the wood it was made of.

Steve's heart was racing with adrenaline. If Billy or Luke walked out of the motel door, he would be caught in the back of the car with nowhere to go. Certain death would follow.

Just as Steve crawled to the back and got into position to pull the back seat down to gain entry to the trunk, a dog began barking across the street. Why the dog started barking was to be seen. The animal probably saw a harmless rabbit hop in front of him.

Steve froze as the lights in the motel room came on. He dove to the floor of the backseat. Between the cracks in the seat, he could see Billy coming out of the motel room.

Billy listened to the dog barking and peered into the early morning darkness trying to see why. He lit a cigarette as he watched the driveway.

Steve held his breath and did not move a muscle. Billy was just a few feet from the front of the car. The slightest movement would draw his attention to the Lincoln with Steve hiding in the backseat.

"See anything?" Luke called from in the room.

"Naw it's nothing. Dumb dog is probably barking at the wind."

Steve sighed in relief as he saw the motel door close behind Billy. The intensity of the encounter caused Steve to break into a sweat that dripped from his forehead onto his eyelids.

Steve went back to work on lowering the back seat to gain access to the gold. He lowered it enough to crawl from the inside of the car to the trunk. He fumbled around until he found a way to release the trunk lid from the inside. As he released it, a dull pop could be heard.

Steve froze in his position. He hoped Billy had not heard it. He did not want him to come outside again. Steve stayed in that position for a few minutes waiting to make sure all was clear.

He was now ready to make his move. He climbed out of the trunk and looked back inside. The gold glimmered in the faint nighttime light. Steve's hunch was right. Billy and Luke had stolen the gold. There it was, in all of its glory, right in front of his eyes.

Steve was going to have to transfer the gold to his car. The only way to do that was to do it two bricks at a time. That is all he could carry. He had to walk approximately fifty yards to where he had parked his car.

He placed a rag on the trunk locking mechanism so he could lower the trunk lid with each trip. He did not want to leave the lid up in case Billy or Luke should glance out the window.

Steve carried the first two bricks to his car successfully. He placed them on the back seat floor until he had a chance to open the trunk of his car. He found a spare key in the ashtray that opened the car's trunk. He removed the two bricks from the back seat and placed them in the trunk.

He turned to head back for another two bricks when the door of the motel room suddenly flew open. Billy ran out with pistol in hand and Luke closely followed him.

Steve had been discovered! They must have heard the noises Steve made as he was opening trunks and walking through the parking lot.

The two men did not immediately see Steve parked off to the left and out of sight. Steve slowly and quietly closed the lid of the trunk. He then slipped into the driver's seat and had the ignition wires in hand should he have to make a quick getaway.

Billy walked around to the back of the Lincoln and saw the trunk ajar.

"Luke, we had a visitor. The darn trunk is open. Looks like whoever it was came in through the back seat. I don't think they got away with anything. It looks like it's all still here."

"Billy, we need to get out of here now!" Luke said.

Billy caught a slight glimmer of the bumper from Steve's sedan. He cocked his head to the right as if looking around a wall. He started to move toward Steve with his gun drawn.

Steve was not waiting. He tapped the two wires together, starting the car, and stomped on the accelerator.

As he fish tailed the car around, rocks spewed in Billy's direction from the tires. Billy ran after the car firing his pistol at Steve. The cloud of dust from Steve's car kept Billy from taking aim.

Luke was already in the car and had the big Lincoln fired up. He backed the car from the parking stall and headed to where Billy was standing and emptying his gun at Steve's car.

Luke pulled up alongside Billy and yelled, "Get in!"

Billy yelled at Luke, "That's my car! That's the car I left in Trinidad. Catch that guy!"

Both men raced out of the motel drive in hot pursuit of Steve who was already on the highway.

"Don't lose him Luke!"

Both cars neared 100 miles per hour as the big Lincoln barreled down on Steve's sedan. Billy fired at Steve from the passenger window with every opportunity he had of an open shot.

The road began to wind through the woods. Both drivers drove on the edge of out of control. Steve had the advantage. His suspension held the road tighter than the Lincoln did. The gold in the back of the Lincoln caused the big car to sway more.

Steve pulled away from Billy and Luke. He had put enough distance between the two cars that he could not be seen by the Lincoln. He found a small road that jutted to the right off the main drag. He made a quick swing to the right and pulled up behind the trees, out of sight from the main road.

He turned the car off and listened. Within moments he heard the roar of the Lincoln pass by. He could tell by the fading noise the Lincoln had sped beyond where Steve was hidden. He had successfully out maneuvered the other two. However, he had not accomplished what he set out to do by taking the gold from Billy and Luke. He had started though. He had two bricks with twenty-three more to go.

CHAPTER 12

Highway 20 - Clear Lake, California
Saturday 7:40 a.m. (PST) - 1962

Luke pulled the Lincoln into the roadside café parking lot. Before stashing the gold at the hideaway, they decided to have breakfast and Billy had to check in with Jake.

The parking lot was to the side of the building out of sight from the patrons eating. Luke parked the car away from all the others. He did not want anyone snooping around while the two men ate.

Steve, hot on the trail of the two men again, came to a fork in the road. He had to make a guess as to which way the Lincoln went. Did they take Highway 101 or Highway 20 just outside of Clear Lake? Highway 20 was a bit winding but had a more direct route to Lake Tahoe. He gambled with his decision and chose to follow Highway 20.

Steve pulled into a gas station just outside of Clear Lake to use the restroom. The area was fairly desolate. He was trying to track down the Lincoln as quickly as he could.

The station attendant was an older man. He appeared to be in his late fifties, dressed in greasy overalls, but still as spry as ever.

Steve asked the station attendant, "Say listen, I've been traveling with some friends of mine and we kind of got separated. You didn't see a black Lincoln come through here lately, did ya?"

"Young fella, you just missed 'em. They stopped about five minutes ago asking for a good place to eat."

"Oh really." Steve said.

"Yep, told 'em there was a café just up the road about two miles. If ya hurry, ya'll catch 'em."

Steve told the attendant thanks and jumped in the sedan. He needed to catch up to Billy and Luke. Steve did not want to lose them again.

Luke and Billy sat in the booth next to the pay phone. Both ordered the breakfast special and coffee. Billy walked to the register, handed the server two one-dollar bills, and asked her for change for the phone. She took the bills, counted out his change, and laid it on the counter. Billy scooped the change into his hand.

Billy took a sip of his coffee as he walked past the booth where the men were sitting. He pondered one last time about the story he would relay to Jake. He then went to the pay phone to make the call.

Steve slipped into the parking lot unnoticed. He parked down and away from the Lincoln. Steve put the car in park and wondered what his next move would be. He certainly could not transfer the gold in broad daylight. That would be too risky.

Steve tried to reason the two men's game plan. He decided that they would take the empty crate to Jake pleading foul by Samantha and him. That seemed reasonable, but what about the gold? They could not just roll up to Jake's place with a trunk full of gold?

Steve figured they would stash the gold somewhere and show up with just the empty crate. A plan was beginning to formulate in his mind about what Billy and Luke might do.

Billy dialed Jake's number at the Cal Neva Casino. Before the call went through the telephone operator instructed him to deposit 35¢ for three minutes. He did as he was told.

"Hey Jake, its Billy."

"So did you find Samantha?" Jake asked.

"No, sure didn't. Her pickup truck was gone from the Eureka Airport. No telling which direction she went."

"I guess no sign of the gold either, huh?"

"No, but I'm bringing you the empty crate. I didn't want to leave it behind. Someone may question seeing it filled with sand and a busted lock. But I did leave the sandbags behind."

Jake was angry.

"When I catch whoever did this they will wish they had never been born!"

"I know Jake. We all did our jobs. The plane made every checkpoint. But it all fell apart with Samantha."

Jake became irritated with this news.

"I will find Samantha. I will make her pay for what she has taken from me. I will take her apart piece by piece. Now get your butts back here...pronto! You're going to hunt down whoever stole that gold from me. It can't be far away."

Billy hung up the phone feeling confident in making Samantha and Steve look bad in Jake's mind. He sat back down in the booth just as his breakfast was placed on the table.

Luke asked, "All okay? Jake buying it?"

Billy smiled and simply said, "Oh yeah."

Steve was still in the parking lot putting his plan together. He somehow had to get his hands on the gold and yet alert Jake to the fact that Billy masterminded the theft.

Steve thought of the two gold bricks in the trunk of his sedan and had an idea. He found a pen and paper in the car's backseat. He quickly scratched a note. It read:

Looking for the gold? Why is there one brick still in the crate? Seems a little odd, wouldn't you say? Better have a heart to heart with Billy. He knows something.

Steve took the note and one gold brick from the trunk of his car. He quickly made his way across the parking lot to the Lincoln. He was in luck. Luke did not lock his door.

Steve crawled inside the Lincoln and lifted the lid off the crate in the back seat. A couple of loose sandbags were still in the bottom. Steve cleared the sandbags to the side, laid the note on the bottom, and placed the gold brick on top of it. He then covered both with the empty sandbags.

He was hoping Billy and Luke would leave the crate untouched until they saw Jake. It was not that far to the Cal Neva from where they were.

Steve returned to his car and parked so he was hidden from the sight of the Lincoln. He would be able to see them leave when they entered the road from the café.

Billy and Luke finished their breakfast, paid, and walked to the Lincoln. They were headed for the Cal Neva Casino and it was going to be an important stop for them. They were to see Jake. Luke pulled the Lincoln onto the highway. Steve slipped out behind them. He once again was following them at a distance.

Highway 20 - Nice, California
Saturday 8:10 a.m. (PST) - 1962

Luke slowed the Lincoln to see what side roads were coming up.

"No...I don't think it's this one Luke. The road had three tall pines on the northwest corner. Drive a little further."

Luke slowly drove on. Steve followed out of sight behind the two.

"There it is. Turn left here."

The two men drove onto a side dirt road and headed into the woods. Steve followed them. He saw a small opening that he could drive off the main path and back into the woods. He turned the sedan onto the path and brought it to a stop behind a clump of bushes, out of sight from Billy and Luke.

Steve got out of his car and crept up to where the two men had pulled up to an abandoned hunting shack.

"Over there Luke. That's where we'll put it."

Billy retrieved a couple of shovels from the tool shed. Steve saw both men start digging a hole twenty feet behind the outhouse. The dirt was soft so the digging was swift.

After the men dug a hole about four feet deep, they threw the shovels aside.

Out of breath and huffing, Billy told Luke, "Okay, back the car up to the hole and we'll finish the job."

Luke did as Billy had instructed. He stopped the rear of the Lincoln short of the hole and opened the trunk.

Billy took an old white sheet from the car and laid it in the hole with one edge draping over the mound of dirt they had just dug from the ground. Next, Luke began handing Billy the bricks of gold and Billy stacked them in the hole on top of the sheet.

Billy was standing with his hands held out after Luke handed him the twenty-third brick. Luke began rummaging through the trunk.

"Come on Luke give me the last two bricks so we can get out of here."

"There isn't any more Billy!"

"What do you mean, there isn't any more?"

Luke sarcastically answered, "Just like I said…there isn't any more."

"Listen Luke. When I sent you to that plane to switch the gold with the sandbags there were twenty-five bricks. Now what did you do with the other two?"

Billy was starting to get hostile with Luke. He went for his gun to emphasize his point. Luke just gave a smile and a laugh as he answered.

"You little weasel! Who do you think you are pulling a gun on? Huh? Me? Did you forget about the letters I sent for my protection? Maybe Jake would like to hear what happened to his gold? So my little hot headed friend…go ahead and pull the trigger because if you do, you're pulling it on yourself!"

Billy just stared at him. He wanted to pull it but he could not be sure if Luke was bluffing or not. He finally put the gun back in his holster.

He sighed as he said, "Whoever was driving my car back at the motel must have known we had the gold and took two bricks. It's a good thing we interrupted whoever it was or they may have gotten off with all of it. Come on, let's cover this up and get out of here."

The men pulled the sheet over the top of the gold and shoveled the dirt back in the hole. They placed the rim to a toilet seat from an old outhouse over the pile to mark the spot.

Billy dusted himself off and said, "Okay, let's go see Jake."

Luke said, "Wait."

He fished in his pocket and pulled out a silver medallion with the Cal Neva logo on it. Next, he went to the tool shed and grabbed a hammer and a nail. He went to the tree directly behind where the gold was buried. Luke pushed the tall grass aside and nailed the medallion to the base of the tree. He let the grass flop back in place hiding the medallion.

"There, if for some reason our toilet seat marker is moved, we can still find where the gold is buried by searching for that medallion."

Steve watched from the bushes as the Lincoln pulled away from the hunting shack. He watched it disappear down the dirt road on its way to the main highway.

Steve contemplated digging the gold up. He could get it now and be on his way, but to where? He did not belong here. How was he going to get back?

He decided he needed to see this thing play itself out. He would go to the Cal Neva and see if it would help him answer some questions before taking the gold.

Steve pulled from behind the bushes and headed for the main road. He no longer needed to stalk the Lincoln. He knew where it was headed. He just needed the Lincoln with Billy and Luke in it to arrive first.

Cal Neva Casino - Lake Tahoe, California
Saturday 11:12 a.m. (PST) - 1962

The Lincoln pulled into the rear of the Cal Neva Casino. The story line had been rehearsed repeatedly by the two men. Samantha and Steve were getting the blame for stealing the gold and the two goons, Billy and Luke, had the story down pat.

Luke turned the Lincoln off. The men paused before getting out of the car.

"Luke, what happened out there in the woods...well I was just nervous, okay?"

"Billy, you are such a piece of dirt! You weren't nervous. You are greedy. You thought I took that gold. You think I am going to steal the gold. You are...ah, you're not worth it. Let's just get this over with."

The two men walked into Jake's office. He was on the phone when they arrived.

"Giovanni...but Giovanni...I know. Listen I'm going to get to the bottom of this. No...well yeah...but...okay Giovanni. I understand."

Jake hung up the phone, grabbed the cord, and ripped it from the wall. He threw the phone across the room narrowly missing Billy. Jake was enraged with the phone call he had just had with Giovanni.

He screamed at Billy and Luke.

"Do you know who that was? Do you? I have been handed my rear on this one. Giovanni is holding my organization responsible. It was my people that screwed it up. I can assure you...someone is going to pay for this!"

"With all due respect Jake, it wasn't our people. It was that pilot. He somehow enticed Samantha to turn on us."

Steve pulled into the Cal Neva general parking while Jake was seething with anger and having his heated discussion with Billy and Luke. He parked so that he would have a clear view of what he hoped was Jake's private entrance.

There he waited. He was not sure what he was waiting for but he expected something to happen.

Inside, Billy continued with his lies.

"They blew Frankie's car sky high with him in it at the Eureka Airport. It looks like they used the explosives from the plane to do it."

"What about Tony? Where is Tony?" Jake asked.

Billy was getting nervous. Jake had that affect on people. He explained another lie to the big man.

"Well after we got to Trinidad and discovered what happened, Lester and Tony got into an argument. One thing led to another. Soon there was pushing and shoving. Tony slammed Lester into his car and somehow it knocked the gearshift in drive.

"Lester's shirt got caught up on the car while it was rolling toward the cliff. Tony saw what happened and tried to run after him and untangle Lester's shirt. It didn't work. He couldn't free him.

"He ran around to the driver's side and jumped in to hit the brakes but it was too late. They went over the edge all the way to the bottom. Poor Tony was just trying to save Lester and the car took both of them to their deaths."

Billy thought it might help to bring the crate in to help prove Steve and Samantha were the culprits. He whispered to one of Jake's henchman to retrieve the crate from the backseat of the Lincoln.

Steve saw a man walk out of Jake's office entrance. He observed the man walk to the Lincoln and pull the wooden crate from the back seat. Steve was hoping his plan of planting the gold brick and the letter was going to work. The crate appeared to be on its way to Jake's office. Time would soon tell.

Steve looked to the right to make sure he was not in sight of anyone coming. Just as he was about to look back to the left, a blast shattered the driver's door window sending glass shards cascading in on Steve's lap.

Steve, startled and confused, looked to see the thug that pulled him from the car at the Cal Neva the day before standing there. He had taken his fist and rammed it into the glass.

He grabbed Steve by both hands and yanked him through the open window. The power of the big man was useless to fight against.

"Someone wants to see you Mr. Pilot Buddy," the big man laughingly quipped.

He manhandled Steve down the walkway and into the doorway. Steve recognized the hallway as the one that led to Jake's office.

Fear was setting in. Steve was not sure the truth would come out before he was killed. In his mind he questioned...*could this really be happening? Would he find himself back in present time as had happened before or would he be a casualty in 1962 and never see the life he left?*

The big man pushed Steve through the door and into Jake's office. He stumbled to the floor. Jake shadowed over him. He reared back and kicked Steve in the groin making him double over in pain.

"You steal from me! No one steals from Jake. Now where's my gold?"

"I don't have your gold. Why don't you ask Billy?" Steve shouted as he agonized in pain.

Billy looked stunned. He had to find a way to shut Steve up. If he didn't, he was going to lose control of the situation.

Jake was becoming even more enraged.

"Check with Billy? Why should I check with him? You and Samantha are the ones who stole the gold right out from under me!"

Jake was so upset he kicked the crate. The lid went flying as the crate fell over. Once it did, the gold brick and the note Steve had written fell out of the crate onto the floor.

Billy and Luke were stunned. They looked at each other as if they had seen a ghost. They had no clue what had happened.

Jake reached down and picked up the gold brick and the note. He too had no clue as to what was happening. He read the note aloud.

Looking for the gold? Why is there one brick still in the crate? Seems a little odd, wouldn't you say? Better have a heart to heart with Billy. He knows something.

Jake looked at Steve and then at Billy.

"Billy, what's the meaning of this?" Jake asked.

Billy went into a rage and lunged at Steve. He put his hands around Steve's throat and squeezed hard. He was yelling and cursing at Steve. Billy now knew he was setup by Steve and possibly Samantha too. He was going to get his revenge on Steve for doing this.

Steve felt the air leaving his lungs. He tried to fight off the hands of Billy around his neck but he could not quite grasp the man the way his body was positioned. Billy squeezed harder.

Steve felt the life going out of him. In the background, he could still hear Billy cursing but the noise was becoming very distant. He felt as though he were flying through the air but yet motionless. The noise became less and less until silence filled his ears.

Six Months Later
1962

Things changed that day back in 1962. Billy had a serious chokehold on Steve and was ready to squeeze the last bit of life out of him when suddenly Steve just vanished. No explanation...just vanished into midair.

Six months later some off-road vehicles out four wheeling found two badly burned and mutilated bodies in the Nevada desert. They turned out to be the bodies of Billy and Luke.

Jake discovered the truth that day. The truth that Samantha and Steve did not steal the gold but it was Billy all along that masterminded the theft for which Jake made Billy pay dearly.

Samantha disappeared from the crime family she was associated with. After that night in Eureka with Steve, she went back to her Minneapolis home and worked at raising a family. Her husband never found out about her stint with the mob.

She raised two beautiful daughters. Years later, her daughter had a daughter of her own...April Thompson.

It was not long after that the mob finally did catch up to her and Samantha disappeared like so many others. Although it was years before the mob found her, she still knew too much to let her just walk. Some say she ended up at the bottom of Lake Michigan. Others say she was buried alive in a Wisconsin forest. Her body was never found.

Shortly after the gold heist, Jake had a review with the Nevada Gaming Commission. During an audit, too many improprieties had been discovered. Payoffs no longer worked and Jake lost his gaming license at the Cal Neva Casino.

Jake ended up in San Quentin for racketeering and extortion. To this day, he is still there, living out a life sentence. Turns out, he did not have as many friends as he thought he did.

The Cal Neva Casino sat vacant for a few years before it was demolished to build a strip mall. A young land developer who had become an icon in the area for building businesses designed and built it.

It all started one day for him with an old white sedan he bought for pennies on the dollar during an auction of things left behind at the old Cal Neva Casino. The car had a busted left driver's door window and the ignition was hotwired.

Seems when he got the old car home, in the trunk he found a lone brick of gold. The sale of that gold brick gave him the needed funds to jump-start a business idea he had for the area. He took that business and parlayed it into a business empire that still thrives today.

The Russian shooters scheduled to assassinate JFK packed up and left Washington, DC once they heard from Krill that the whole operation was a bust. However, Krill was not satisfied with the deaths of just Vinnie, Don Carlo, and Little Al. He wanted the top. He sent the hit team to New York.

Giovanni was found dead in a back alley. Indications showed it was Russian made weapons that took him down. No one ever confirmed the source of the weapons. No one even cared.

In the river off Highway 36 in the Trinity National Forest of Northern California, a fly fisherman hooked a branch. He waded over to the downed tree and after brushing the branches aside, found a badly decomposed body entangled underneath.

The identification found on the body was badly weathered from the elements. The name of Tony was barely visible on his driver's license. Everyone thought it must have just been a drifter and he was buried in an unmarked grave.

The undergrowth grew up and around the old toilet seat on that dusty road off Highway 20 in Northern California. Maybe the gold was still buried there and maybe it wasn't. One thing for sure, it cursed everyone who touched it.

The FBI in Washington, DC continued its monitoring of the mob movements. Nothing ever came of the Senator's meetings with Lou. The FBI was about to close down the investigation until that day in November 1963 that rocked the world for years to come. The assassination of the President that year was enough to keep the investigation open.

No one understood how Steve simply vanished that day back in Jake's office. Not even Steve. He just knows the world went dark, his breathing stopped, and then the transformation. How, why, or what triggered it remained a mystery at the time.

CHAPTER 13

Lake Tahoe Airport, California
Thursday 10:18 a.m. (PST) - Present Day

George Masters was watching and admiring the grace of the *Curtiss Helldiver* on final approach to Runway 18 at the Lake Tahoe Airport. He was proud of the restoration work he had completed on the plane.

Steve had been up testing the plane for a good part of an hour. He wondered if Steve would purchase the plane when he returned to the ground. Steve, piloting the plane, pondered how he would use it in his charter aircraft business.

He had the plane aligned with the runway on final approach when it struck. It was as if light exploded around him just by flipping the switch to extend the flaps for the landing.

George, watching from the ground, seeing but not believing his eyes, was mortified at what had just happened! Three large Canadian Geese flew out of nowhere directly into the pilot canopy. The impact was so violent it shattered just about every inch of the canopy glass. Jagged shrouds flew everywhere.

Steve heard the explosion but did not see it. However, he did have the presence of glass falling in on him. He had briefly glanced down to set the flaps for landing when it happened. He tried to get the plane to respond or at least he thought he had.

The gasket sealing the canopy to the plane had let loose from the bird impact and had flown back and wrapped around Steve's neck. The blood flow to his head was severely restricted. Soon he lost consciousness.

George watched helplessly as he saw the plane dip from side to side. He knew Steve was in trouble. He could see the canopy smashed and pieces of the plane dangling from the impact. What looked like blood seemed everywhere. George was not sure if it was from Steve or the birds.

Remarkably, the plane seemed to stay on course for landing. George had hope that maybe Steve was okay.

The plane continued to get lower and lower. Finally, the wheels skimmed the runway, bounced once, and then came down hard. The plane glided down the runway. The engine was silent as was everything else except for the sound of the emergency vehicle sirens headed for the plane.

The first rescue workers on the scene quickly jumped into action. They could see Steve was being strangled by the gasket wrapped tightly around his neck.

The rescue worker that climbed to the canopy area first quickly cut the cord from around Steve's neck to clear his windpipe. The air flooded Steve's gasping lungs. His color returned to his face and he began to cough and gasp for more air. The rescue worker had saved his life that day.

Steve opened his eyes to see the commotion. He saw the jagged canopy that just a few minutes ago was a perfect bubble of protection.

Once Steve's eyes refocused, the first thing he saw was the etching on the dash *ST MPLS 62*. He rubbed his fingers across it feeling the edges and wondered. *Could it be possible? Had it happened again?*

Just moments prior to the gasket being removed from around Steve's neck, he was in Jake's office being strangled by Billy.

Time travel had happened twice now. However, a pattern was emerging, a pattern that may hold the secret to Steve's future.

Lake Tahoe, California - Community Hospital
Friday 11:00 a.m. – Present Day

Julie quickly caught a flight to Lake Tahoe at the news of the accident. She worried for Steve's safety.

She arrived at his hospital room and was relieved to see Steve sitting up and talking. He was a little battered from the debris field that rained in on him but for the most part, he was okay. He saw Julie and her worried look.

He smiled and said, "Hey gorgeous. At least I'm better off than the birds that hit me."

"Mr. Mitchell, I swear I am going to take your airplane toys away from you if it's the last thing I do."

Both laughed.

Once the room had cleared, he motioned Julie to come close to him. He spoke softly. He did not want anyone to hear.

"I know what was in that wooden crate. I saw it firsthand. Not only do I know what was in it but also I know what it was going to be used for. I'm not sure it ever made it but with the way world events turned out in the 60's, I have an idea it did."

Julie looked puzzled and bewildered.

"What in the world are you talking about Steve?"

He continued, "I don't know how or why, but the last few minutes of that landing after the bird strike...I was in another dimension again. I saw the wooden crate I had in my first plane crash. I was back in time again!"

"Steve, are you sure it wasn't just your injuries?"

"Julie, it happened. I know it did. I was back in 1962 and the mob was planning a hit on…get this…JFK!"

"Steve you're scaring me."

"No, you don't need to be scared. What I am telling you is true. I'll prove it to you. I'll take you to the places I have been. I'll research the people I met back then. I'll show you proof on that plane. I cannot explain how it happened but it did. I have some real investigative work to do. I may just be onto something with the JFK assassination."

"Well Steve there is no doubt your life certainly is adventurous."

"Yes it is," Steve replied, "and I have a lot of questions to ask but first things first. Would you get me my cell phone please? I think the nurses put it in the cabinet over there. I've got an important call to make."

Julie rummaged through his belongings the hospital had placed in the cabinet opposite Steve's bed. She found Steve's phone and handed it to him. He dialed the number for George Masters.

"Hey George, Steve here. Sorry about what happened to the plane but I want to buy it anyway.…Yes, I'll pay the price.…No, don't worry about it. In the short time of flying it I've come quite attached to it.… thanks, I'll see you then."

Steve had made up his mind to purchase the plane. He knew it held a wealth of clues that he hoped would lead to answers to his questions.

Steve laid the phone down by his bedside. He turned to Julie who was looking out the window. Somehow, he knew his life crossed her path for a reason. He was not going to let that go.

"Hey Julie."

She turned and answered, "Yes Steve."

"I know you make good money at the hospital and all, but...would you ever consider leaving?"

"For what?" she asked.

"Well I've been thinking. We kind of happened into dating and this may defy logic, but would you consider going to work for me?"

"Now Steve…I can't fix a plane, I can't fly one, and I'm no sales person. What on earth would I do for you?"

"I'm not talking about my charter business. I want you with me. I want you to help me track down whatever it was I just experienced. It was real. I know it was. There is a trail of bloodshed and gold that I need to resolve if not for the country but for myself.

"Look at what happened from my first crash. No one can explain that I visited the 1860's, but I did. We have the proof in that wooden plane carving. My great grandfather, who I had never met, planned for his future relatives he would never know. How did he know to do that if I had not visited him when he was a little boy?

"Yes, what's happened to me is real. What I saw in the past has enormous impact on this country. I need to track down some events and people I just experienced and I want you with me to help. Would you please…I'll pay you more than what you make at the hospital."

Julie turned and looked out the window again while pondering his proposal. After a moment, she turned back to Steve.

"Do I get to keep my benefits?"

"You sure do! Whatever medical, dental, vacation time…whatever it is you have now, you will get with me."

"Steve…I'm not talking about my benefits with the hospital."

She smirked as she moved closer to him.

"I'm talking about my benefits with you."

Steve opened his arms to her and as they hugged, he simply said, "You bet!"

Highway 20 - Nice, California
Late Fall - 1962

The three tall pines swayed slightly in the breeze. The night air was crisp and fresh. Moonlight filtered through the trees casting shadows on the forest floor.

A vehicle slowed as it approached the dusty trail next to the pines. It gingerly turned down the dirt road with its lights off. The vehicle left a small dust trail as it ventured deeper into the woods. It stopped at the end of the trail next to the old abandoned hunting shack.

A figure emerged from the vehicle and slithered along in the darkness. The person retrieved a shovel from the back of the vehicle. The individual stepped carefully, dodging the moonlight until arriving at the mound of dirt off the beaten path.

The toilet seat made a swooshing sound as it was tossed aside and landed in the tall grass next to the base of a tree. The shovel scooped the soft dirt aside. With each shovel full, the individual got closer to the payoff. Soon the sheet was pulled back. The gold still glimmered in the night light.

Swiftly, each bar of gold was carefully loaded into the vehicle. Time was quickly passing and the job was soon completed. The vehicle left as mysteriously as it came. The road was dark that night but darker were the intentions of the individual in that vehicle.

THE END

To be continued in

The Mystery of the Missing Gold

Printed in the United States
by Baker & Taylor Publisher Services